QUEEN CANARY

Simone Saves the World
Among Other Things

Tara Cargle Ashcraft

"*The movers and shakers on our planet, aren't the billionaires and generals, they are the incredible numbers of people around the world filled with love for neighbor and for the earth who are resisting, remaking, restoring, renewing and revitalising.*"

BILL MCKIBBEN

CHAPTER ONE

Monday, August 26

I bolt upright and knock my head *hard* on the bottom bunk. Tears stream down my face. My breath is ragged. My heart thumps heavy in my chest. This is bad. This is very, very bad. My head is killing me and it's not just from banging it on the wooden beam above me. I kick my legs and pound my arms into my blankets. No. No. NO. NO. NO. I kick until my muscles ache. Inside I'm screaming bloody murder, but I don't actually make a sound. I can't scare my parents or even my dog for that matter. Not now. Not at 6 AM. Not after what I've put them through. Not after the last year.

I can't believe I had another one. Why now? Things have been so much better. I've been better. I'm getting better. I ~~will at the realization of what happened during the night~~. I close my eyes and count to ten. I focus on my breath until it feels normal again. My therapist taught me to inhale on a slow four count and exhale for five even longer ones. Breathe. It's weird to have to think about doing something that your body is supposed to do all on its own, but I'm getting used to it.

I lay back down and think about the dream. More like a nightmare really. I'm haunted by it. I shudder at the thought ~~of it~~. I pull my Carolina blue covers to my chin. I need com-

3

fort. The memory of the dream is bleary, brown, and broken. A prosperous blue, green, and white Earth is nearly gone. It's been replaced with its own carcass. An empty, lifeless shell of a planet. An abandoned exoskeleton. Thick, coal colored clouds hover around the citizens like they are real life Pig Pens. There are no more waves to jump, but polluted, inky water fills the crumbling streets. No rainbow colored fish. Lost cities. Overcrowded temporary housing. The people and animals are baking in a relentless heat so dense and hot, it's like being smothered with a flannel blanket on the Solstice. Snippets of the starving, dejected people standing in endless lines waiting for rationed food and water settle in the corners of my mind. I'm alarmed at the thought of no fresh food and not clean enough water to drink. I kick my legs again in frustration. I pound my fists in fear.

What am I supposed to do with this? I feel sick. I might throw up. I probably will by the end of the day; my headache is that ruthless. This is not what I need right now. School's just started. I've been really happy. Really content. My eyes fill up. I'm so pissed that this has happened again. Why can't I be normal? I look at the clock. I need to get going. I have to move. I have to *keep* going. I have to act normal, at least for now. I have no choice. I have to *look alive* as my mom says. I have to look alive because I am alive. Hard to take that for granted when you've glimpsed the alternative. Why? Why me? Why again? I lay back down. My parents will be up soon. They will be calling for me to join them to eat. They will panic if I'm not immediately responsive, although I don't blame them. I can do this. I have to.

With trepidation and commitment, I start my daily routine. I think about Dr. A and her advice. That is what Dr. A would say if she was here, "do what you know until you know what's next." Start with what you know. Start with what has worked in the past. I find my journal buried beneath my t-shirt collection, some dirty and some clean. They are stacked beside my bed. The pen is still stuck between the pages I wrote before I went to sleep last night. So naïve as to what the morning would hold. I note the date and time of the dream. I describe it in detail. I note my symptoms. Anxious sweating. Unrelenting headache. Ragged breath. I consider who should know about this. These are all things the doctors and scientists on my team will want to know. I jot down some possibilities. I try not to panic. I'm better now. I have the tools I need to get through this. I know I won't make it through school with this headache though. I need my mom for that one.

On cue, I hear her calling for me from downstairs. She lets me know it's time to eat. She waits anxiously, as always, for me to respond. "I'm up, Mom. I'm up. Coming down in a few." I steady my voice, filtering out my irritation and fear.

I'm starving. As usual. The thought of food, my grumbling belly, and my mom's insistence, motivate me to pull myself together and follow the smell of frying bacon. I smell the rich, blackness of coffee too. The chicory kind like my grandparents make. The promise of sizzling, fatty deliciousness helps me shrug off the hangover of another terrible, life-changing dream. A Big One. A bad one. I slowly climb out of bed and make my way to the kitchen. Act normal, Simone. Remember to smile. Try and be the first to hug her. Be the kind of daughter a mom wants. Be the kind of kid a dad is proud of. Be normal.

My mom stands at the counter flipping bacon and watching the morning news. President Robinson stands at a podium and speaks with authority as she once again discredits another scientific report about the climate crisis. My mother stops her flipping for a moment and shakes her head in disbelief. My mom is a nurse and loves all things medical and science. She says the only good thing about President Robinson's position on climate change is that it gives her job security because people are getting sicker every year because of it. Until last year, this used to be somewhat funny (although not that much because my mom is not funny on purpose). At the memory, my Guilt Dragon tries to rear his big, ugly, loud-mouthed head. I close my eyes and count to ten. Slowly. Carefully. Thoughtfully. Deep breath in, deep breath out. I watch my mom and know what she's going to say next because she says the same thing every morning.

"Mark my words, Simone Alice Marker, mark my words. If we don't fix this climate problem right now, we are doomed. Doomed, I tell you. All of us. Even Cherry Garcia." He lifts his head from his dog bed and tilts it quizzically at his name. Like, don't bring me into this, lady. "Someone needs to stop this madwoman before she ruins us all. I thought we had a better chance with our first ever non-partisan president, but I'm losing hope by the day. By the day." She adds the last part as if the first by the day weren't enough clarification of the timing she has in mind. She waves her spatula around for additional flair and effect. Beads of bacon fat fly through the air. I see them sparkle in the morning light streaming through the cracked window. I'm thankful for the fresh air. Breathe. Be normal. My stomach growls again at the sight of the tiny, fatty bubbles.

Well, maybe she doesn't say that exact thing every single day, but something like it. To the effect. I don't even know why she bothers to watch the news anymore anyways. It's a *real* positive start to the day. I'm two weeks into my sophomore year, and every day I'm "inspired" by my mom's reaction to the morning news. I grab a fistful of bacon off the plate she sits in front of me along with one little blue and white pill. I need something more though. The ache in my head is making it hard to see straight. I'm starting to get a picture in picture, double exposure, of what I see around me. Not a good sign.

I have to be careful though. This is a very fine line. I can't act like my headache is super bad, not like Big One bad, or she will freak out. I also can't ask for heavy meds without a good reason because, as we have seen, I can't be trusted with lots of pills. Not when I'm maddened with crippling pain and depression that is. She won't suspect the depression part. I've been much, much better lately, but if I let on about a really bad headache, she's going to suspect something more than I want to talk about right now. I also can't say something like I *think* I *might* be getting a headache because that will make me look pill greedy. I go for straightforward and non-dramatic. I won't get the good stuff that will know it out completely, and prevent it from taking over my entire body, but I'll get something to manage the pain until I get home from school. I hope.

"Hey, Mom. I have a headache. Just like a regular headache. Probably period related." I throw up my hands to indicate the injustice of it all. The erratic move jars my head and makes it throb even more. She eyes me warily.

"Simone Alice Marker, are you okay? What's wrong? What's going on? How are you feeling, really? Did you have a dream?" She's walking towards me like she's going to tackle me to the ground if I give a wrong answer to her litany of questions.

"Mom," I push my arm out as a preventative stop to her attack. "I'm okay, Mom. Calm down." Oh, she hates that. Bad choice of words. Bad move. I keep going so she doesn't protest the error of my teenage ways. "I'm fine. Really. I just have a headache, and I have a big day today. I just need to be able to focus. That's all." I point towards my belly to remind her the reason I've touted.

Lies of omission aren't the same as flat out lies. Right? I have to believe that. I don't tell her that I *didn't* have a dream. I just didn't answer her question directly, per se. My belly does a little flip-flop at the acknowledgement of the lie. One point for the Guilt Dragon. She stops advancing towards me and turns back to the locked medicine cabinet. She pulls the key out of her apron pocket and takes out a little white bottle that rattles with, what I'm guessing, is the medium grade painkillers. I really need the high-grav stuff, but I can't go there right now. Maybe these will work better than they used to. Maybe all the work I've been doing on the function of my brain will make my whole head more pain resistant. I cross my fingers. When you're psychic, you have a lot of superstitions. I wash my blue and white one and the horse pill yellow one down with a forceful swallow.

"Thanks, Mom. I'm fine, really. I'm going to get ready for school. Can't be late!" I add that last part to appeal to her sense of rules and order. Not because I really care that much about timeliness. Know your audience.

I make my way back upstairs before she can stop me. I would run, but I can't risk jostling my head again. It doesn't take me long to throw on my favorite worn-in jeans, mustard yellow Vans, and my dad's old Grateful Dead t-shirt. The real-deal, not the ones from Target. I have standards. I tie the shirt in a knot at the small of my back. I don't want to look like a hobo, just not like the rest of the girls in my grade. I pull it down though to meet the top of my jeans. No need to show off my soft middle to a bunch of idiot classmates with big mouths and lots to say about everybody's body. My hair goes back in a braid down my back. I inspect my face for acne. One giant one. As always. Every day. She just relocates based on the time of the month. Today, Gertrude is sitting on the top of my cheekbone. She's shiny and taut with a snow white head and a red apple bottom. It takes everything in my soul not to pop her. Instead, I dab a little concealer on her. I can't decide if this makes it better or worse, but it's time to go regardless. Oh, the tribulations.

I'm proud of myself for keeping it together for my parents and for Cherry Garcia's sake. He's waiting for me to let him out when I leave for the day. I wish he could go with me, like Elle and Bruiser. Cherry Garcia and my parents might be okay this morning, but my insides are quivering in fear, and my head is not yet responding to the meds doled out by my mom. It's going to be a long day, and I haven't even begun to figure out what I'm supposed to do with the dream. I rub the rabbit's foot (a fake rabbit, I hope to god) in my pocket. For good luck of course. My parents have already left for work. I lock and unlock the door three times. Per my usual routine. All good.

At school, I find Connelly, my best friend forever, waiting for me by my locker as she does every morning. Her dad doesn't let her walk to school with just me anymore. She used to walk to my house and then we'd go together from there. He's very protective of her now that her mom is gone. Dead. Her mom is dead. She didn't just go away. She's not coming back. Again, my Guilt Dragon sticks up a sharp claw. Then another. I silently tell him to stand down. STAND DOWN. I'm using all my crazy-people tools this morning. My therapist says don't say "crazy" but I do. It's the least of my worries. As I approach the locker, Connelly hands me a muffin, my favorite, chocolate chip. She's good to me like that.

"Good morning, SAM," she smiles with her voice and her whole face. She really is the kindest human being that ever lived. She calls me SAM – short for Simone Alice Marker. That's what my mom calls me most of the time. Why not just Simone? Or Simone Alice? Or just Alice? Although, those aren't my favorite nicknames either. My parents call me Queen Canary when I'm upset or anxious or fortune-telling or being all kinds of psychic and what not. That's my favorite name. I picture this beautiful yellow bird with a sparkly golden crown hanging a bit crooked from the high feathers atop its head. Black fierce eyes. Looking out. Ready to warn. The image makes me feel less like a weirdo and more like a sage. A royal sage. I need less weirdo in my life and more normal, beautiful stuff. That's for sure.

"Hi. Thanks for the muffin, Cupcake." I'm acting normal. I'm thinking normal. This is good. Keep it up, Simone. Atta, girl. Be normal. Say what you always say when you see your bestie on a Monday morning. Normal vibes needed.

"What's up, Con-Woman?" Speaking of names, she hates it when I call her that. I don't know why I keep doing it. She doesn't even think it has anything to do with her name, but CONNelly...Con-Woman...I like it. Makes her seem more bad-ass. Although in her defense, there is literally nothing con-like about her. I'm trying to give her edge is all.

"The only con person here is you with all the CONvincing you're doing to get me to go with you to see that medium in D.C. this weekend. What's his name? Dr. McDreamy?" She giggles at her own reference to one of her many TV addictions. "I got your texts, all 21 of them. You know I can't get to the city without my dad finding out, and you know he will never let me go. If you're going, you're going alone, my friend. I still love you though, SAM." She bats her eyes at me dramatically. She indicates the muffin with those same eyes and adds waggling her eyebrows to the mix. As if the muffin is enough to make me feel better. Although it helps. I'll give her that. I'm willing the muffin to make my head feel better too. Chocolate is supposed to ease headache pain. I also need a major dose of caffeine. I need to hit the vending machine before first block. Chocolate and coffee galore before 9 AM. My mom would kill me.

"CONNELLY, his name is not Dr. McDreamy. You watch too much Netflix. He is a doctor of the Pseudosciences, a medium, specializing in dream interpretation, premonitions, and messages from the other side. I don't know why you can't remember that. You know I have to go. You know how much it means to me." I'm definitely whining. Between my head hurting and my disappointment that she's turning me down, the whining is coming easily. Connelly doesn't know this yet, but it's even more important for me to go now after the night I had.

"I have to get going. I need to go by the cafeteria. I can't be late again. Miss Starnes will kill me, but I need to talk to you at lunch. Meet me at the end of A hall so we can get that good table in the atrium. It's not too crowded over there, but loud enough so that everyone won't be all in our business." I roll my eyes to indicate the annoyance of the masses. I can barely get the words out, my head throbs to the beat of the clatter in my head. I pause for a second. I need her to know how serious I am. I touch her elbow. I take a breath.

"Connelly, I had another dream. A Big One." Connelly's face falls from its normal cherub-like cheeriness. I don't know how she can still be so kind and happy after everything she's been though. The last year was just as hard on her as it was on me. Harder, obviously. She's the one with the dead mom. No matter what though, she is like a Happy Warrior, and she just keeps on keeping on. The way we deal with things is very different. I go dark. Music. Silence. Solitude. She goes bright. Boys. Parties. Hobbies. I hate to make her sad, but I have to tell her about last night. Another dream. Another Big One. I've been trying to process what I dreamt, and I need her. I need to talk to her about it. I need her support. She's my best friend. It's not going to be an easy conversation, but it is necessary. She just nods, and I turn to go. Must get caffeine.

My pre-cal teacher is droning on and on about some kind of angles and calculations and other things that make my brain want to jump out of my aching head and run into oncoming traffic. I let my mind drift. I try not to think about last year. At least not often. When I do, I'm battling the Guilt Dragon. Trying to keep that monstrous thing at bay. When I think about what has happened over the past two years, I feel sick. When I think about how bad things got. I feel shame. When I think of the pain I caused Connelly and her dad and my parents and myself, I can barely handle it. It makes me lose my breath and not in the good Beyoncé way. In the way like I can't and don't want to breathe. I'm getting better with it all. Therapy is an anchor. No more pills, well, no more handfuls of pills. Just the prescribed one. No more hospitals. But there is the daily struggle of choosing to focus on good stuff, fun stuff, easy stuff. Being lighter.

Last night threw a serious wrench in my progress. I've had bad headaches all my life. I remember having ones so bad, even in Kindergarten, that I would throw up near the cubbies or on my nap mat. The headaches generally reflect my mood. So, if I'm anxious or depressed, the headaches are worse. If I am having a premonition or have had a dream like a Big One, the headaches are unbearable. It's like the emotion and energy of the psychic activity puts a strain on my actual head. It's as if it's too much commotion for my skull to contain. The more intense my psychic sense is, the more intense the headache is. I can tell the difference between the kinds of headaches I have. The one I have today is not depression or period related for that matter; it is straight up premonition. Last night's dream about the climate crisis is going to come true.

Every night before bed, I know that what I dream that night might be a reality by morning. It's an exhausting truth to live with. It also makes you hyper aware of your dreams and your thoughts. It can be exhausting. I remember every dream I've ever had. I keep track of how many come true. When I have a Big One, my accuracy rate is nearly 100%. I dreamt Hurricane Caroline, the falling of the Hightower Bridge, and the Blackstone National Park Wildfire. I dreamt Flight 215 disappearing into the sky, never to be found. I dreamt the assassination attempt of our last Vice President.

After a while, my parents got me involved with this research study thing. They are a group of scientists and doctors that study precognitive dreaming. They collect dreams from around the globe and aggregate them to look for patterns and signals. For the big events, I at least have a way to warn someone. I tell the Dream Team and let them deal with it. If they have enough people from around the world that tell them a certain activity that is going to happen, then they have ways to intervene. Like with the assassination attempt, over 1,000 psychics dreamt the Vice President's assassination, and the Dream Team was able to get the right resources to prevent it. They found the sniper with his plans and materials before he shot. That was a relief. I felt good about my weirdness that day.

With the Dream Team, I don't feel solely responsible for the damage when a Big One comes true. All of those big events are atrocious and overwhelming, but really what am I going to do to stop a hurricane? When I dream about the death of someone that I know, it's so personal, so singular. Dreaming about something tragic happening to someone you love, is a whole different kind of emotional wreckage.

A year before Connelly's mom was diagnosed with leukemia, I had a horrible, horrible dream. I woke up the same as I did this morning, crying and dysregulated with a pounding headache. In my dream, Mrs. Carpenter got very, very sick and then, well, then, she died. I didn't tell anyone about the dream, not even the Dream Team. I typically tell them the dreams that impact a lot of people or really big crisis type things. I'm not sure why I didn't tell them about Mrs. Carpenter, maybe because it didn't fit the criteria of what they look for? It wasn't a hurricane or an assassin. Also, I think I was so afraid that it would come true that I was paralyzed. I didn't want to say it out loud. I didn't want to give it any more power. It was so personal. I failed. I should've told. I was selfish. I just want to be normal sometimes; maybe I ignore the abnormal. Why didn't I just say something?

As soon as Mrs. Carpenter got sick, I started fighting with the Guilt Dragon. I'd never had such an intense dream about one person before. Normally, my dreams are about big events or nameless (to me) populations of people. Maybe because I thought people would think I'm crazy? Crazier than they already think I am. Dreaming the death of your best friend's mom isn't NORMAL. The Guilt Dragon took over my body and mind like its own kind of cancer. It still haunts me to this day. If I had told Connelly or my mom or my therapist or anyone, then I could have saved her. I know it. My depression and headaches got really, really bad though right after she died. That's how I ended up with the pills and the hospital.

One night I just couldn't take the weight of the guilt. I was so sad. A sadness that felt like an anchor was tying me down so low that I couldn't make it to the surface to get even a breath of air. I was overcome with how sad I was, how terrible I felt. My whole body including my head were riddled with excruciating pain. I didn't think I could face Connelly or her dad again. I couldn't look them in the eye knowing that I had known. I knew it in my bones. I could have stopped it. I could have saved her. I could have told someone, anyone, everyone. Together we could have gotten ahead of the sickness. Early detection. Early intervention. All the things you see on TV that save people from stupid, fucking cancer. I didn't. I didn't say anything. I was silent. Day after day after day.

The night I took the pills, I did so to stop the pain. To dull it all. To be numb. I needed a break from my thoughts and my grief and my guilt. That was my intention, but I knew I was taking too many. I knew I was being careless with my life. Official word was unintentional overdose.

Sometimes I tell people, other than my parents and The Dream Team, about my dreams and sometimes I don't. It's usually uncomfortable for everyone when I do. A lot of people don't believe in premonitions, and they think I'm a freak or a liar or a witch. A witch! Sometimes I think being a witch would be way cooler. They think I just want attention. None of which is true. None of which are very helpful when you're in the tenth grade and you *are* kind of weird and awkward and freaky. You don't really need to add to the list.

But when you've had dreams that come true as long as I have, you believe. And after you've sat silent when you could have taken action, you get loud. I will say something. I will do something. What happened last time with Mrs. Carpenter, will not happen this time with the planet. No one understands the pain I feel every day when I remember that I could have saved Mrs. Carpenter. Maybe no one believes me, but I know the truth.

After the night with the pills and the week in the psych ward, I began seeing Dr. Ambrossini weekly. She doesn't make me do anything, but she *highly suggests* certain activities to help me get and stay better. She suggests that I tell carefully selected people about my dreams, about my guilt, explain how overwhelming it all is. She says I need to be honest with people about how I ended up in the hospital fighting my way back to the Land of the Living. I guess I wasn't done here yet. My body rallied even when my soul felt finished. Dr. A says I need to keep processing what happened. She says it doesn't happen overnight and it doesn't happen once. It's called processing because it's a process. She wants me to release it from my body, to give my body and soul and mind permission to leave it behind. So I do. I told my parents and I told Connelly about the dream I had about her mom. Dr. A encourages me to tell Mr. Carpenter when I'm ready and maybe some other close friends, but I haven't. Not yet. Maybe one day. Maybe not. I'd rather forget about it all and never talk about any of it again. But now, it seems I can't. Last night's dream is bringing the past back to the present.

When I tell Connelly about the dream I have about her mother, I weep. I can barely catch my breath when I confess. My chest is tight and heaving. She tries to absolve me from my guilt; she does the best she can. She is grieving too though. I can't imagine how it makes her feel to think, even if it is just a tiny, tiny bit that things could have been different. That I could have raised my hand, even if it made me look like a freak, and say—Mrs. Carpenter, go get checked out. Go to the doctor. I feel selfish telling her when I did. It's too late. What good is a confession now? What's the point? I guess I trust Dr. A. She's gotten me through a lot. I try and do what she says. She says it's okay to be selfish when you are doing it to heal. Part of the process.

That dream. That haunting, brown, desperate dream. I shudder again at the thought. The dreams are back whether I like it or not. I can't just sit back in silence again. After last night, I don't have a choice. I need to remember last year and how awful it was, and I need to speak up. Now.

Connelly respects my "abilities" and is supportive of my dreams, my premonitions, and me because she's Connelly and she's amazing. She also says they are called a pseudoscience for a reason or a *few* reasons if she's being honest. It's a weird dynamic. She says she believes me or wants to believe me, but if she really does then she has to admit that I killed her mom. That it wasn't just fate or destiny or bad luck or bad medicine or science or whatever, but that I actively played a role in her mom dying of a horrible cancer. Then, how could we be friends? How could we have what we have always had? We have the best friendship in all the world.

We've known each other since kindergarten. We're both only children and our parents let us be raised like sisters. We finish each other's sentences. We can read each other's body language and know what each other is thinking or feeling without any words at all. We hold our own language, secrets, plans, and hopes. We have our own little traditions. Our memories are like the most gorgeous, intricate wedding veil, like the one Meghan wore when she married Prince Harry. The veil trails us wherever we go. It cloaks us in its warmth and nostalgia. It make us laugh until we pee our pants. It announces our arrival and shouts our royal greatness. We are perfect friends, family we choose. The sisters we never had until we had each other. We are the yin and yang. My tall square angles, her short soft curves. My dark, straight hair, her yellow bouncing curls. My dark brooding. Her light extroverting. My t-shirts and jeans, her dresses and skirts. My Dead and her T-Swift. Peanut butter and jelly. Macaroni and cheese. Cookies and milk. We are made for each other.

I wait for Connelly at the good table. I watch her come into the atrium. She smiles at kids we don't like and kids we do like as she makes her way to me. She's just nice like that. When she sees me, I notice that her face clouds just a tiny bit. I automatically frown in return. I'm sure she isn't looking forward to a talk about another dream, a Big One at that. It's a sensitive topic of course. But how can I keep it a secret? How can I be quiet after the past two years? Haven't they taught us anything at all? She plops down and drops her full backpack on the ground next to her. It looks like she's carrying the whole library in that bag. The seams stretch thin. Like something needs to give.

"SAM, what did you dream?" She cuts to the chase. There's just a hint of skepticism in her voice. Or maybe it's annoyance. Or maybe I hear something that isn't there. Through the wall of pain in my head, it's hard to be sure of anything.

I tell her about the desolation of the dream and how everything was brown and muddy and wet and hot. I tell her about the rations and how I had to eat little tan pucks of dry porridge and sometimes there weren't even enough of them to go around. I tell her about the mangy, hungry dogs and the extinction of all the other animals that we love to look up on the internet or go see at The National Zoo. I describe how lifeboats full of sad faced people squished together side by side replaced the Metro. How they floated to work in boats because the roads are flooded. I tell her about the gunmetal gray of the sky, and that even though it was too hot to go outside; there is no sunshine, just a muted gray sky full of heavy black clouds. Gray, brown, black. Gray, brown, black. I tell her about the armed guards with guns the size of mini submarines at every corner due to the absolute chaos of the city. The millions of displaced people without homes or healthcare or water or food. Too few jobs. Too few houses. Masks for covering faces. I tell her about the upheaval of the government and the dysfunction of the whole world. There's no New Orleans or San Francisco. No beaches. Nowhere to go. Nothing to see. No way to get there.

The 1% live in fancy high rises that tower over the city. So high above the flooded streets that they have their own transportation, their own schools, and their own stores. They still have hospitals and medicine. They live a separate, clean, functional life. They avoid the constant destruction caused by drought, floods, typhoons, and earthquakes. They went on without the rest of us. Left us to starve and to die of thirst. Left us with no color. No joy. No hope. Their massive skyscrapers wave in the sky high above the black clouds of smoke and ash. They breathe freely. No masks.

I take a breath and decide whether to keep going or not. I watch her as I talk. She listens carefully and respectfully because she's Connelly and that's how Connelly is. She is distracted though. I can tell by the way she keeps refocusing her eyes on me every few minutes. When I get to the part about New Orleans and how it was completely gone, a whole beautiful historic city that just didn't exist anymore, I choke up a little. No more visits to see my grandparents on the coast. This got her attention. Even though this was the second time I'd cried today, I normally don't. Sometimes I wish I did more, like I did the day I told her about the dream about her mom. There was something therapeutic about the intensity and the intimacy of that cry. I decide to stop talking.

She takes the break in my recounting to jump in. "You're serious about this, SAM? You're really scared? You think the Earth could just implode like that? You think that suddenly there will be no water or food? No animals? No dry land? Seriously, SAM?" She isn't being mean. She's asking with genuine concern, but there's something about her response that is off-putting. I can't put my finger on it. She keeps going. "So, you are saying that everything we hear on the news right now about the climate crisis is real? You believe it? I mean, I know how my dad feels about it, but he's my dad. I think he's a little nuts about everything, not just the environment." She tilts her head to the left and her eyes squint a little as she questions me.

"I am, Conn. I wish I wasn't, but it was so real and so creepy. I woke up crying and with a headache just like I did when I…" I don't finish that sentence. I don't want to bring up her mom again. "Plus, yeah, I hear the news. My mom watches it every morning and she basically tells me that the whole world is doomed if we don't do something right now. Right now. I mean, what if she's right? What if we have the opportunity to save the world and we don't? What if I have the chance to save the world and I don't? I can't miss my chance to do something good, to save someone or something. Not again. I can't ignore this, Connelly. You know…" My voice trails off. I lift my eyes to meet hers. She's watching me with a vague frown.

"It's not your fault my mom died, Simone. You know that. I've told you that a million times. What happened, happened. She got sick. She died. Yes, it sucks. I hate it, but a dream wasn't going to stop her from dying. I know you believe in your dreams and I believe in you. I just think, maybe, you're like putting a little too much into it."

It stung like the world's largest jellyfish attacked my face and then just stayed there splayed across my skin. Connelly always supports me. I know she doesn't always agree with me 100%, but she's always by my side. This feels different, and she calls me Simone. That's 1/3 of what my MOM calls me. Not what Connelly calls me.

"Connelly-It's not the dream that could have saved her it." She interrupts me. "Listen, SAM. I think you should do what you need to do, and I'm here for you. Anytime you want to talk about this or, I don't know, give me an update or whatever. I'm here for it. I'm here for you. But I can't, like, get involved with this. You know how my dad is right now. He's so protective. I can't tell him that I need to help SAM save the world so that the planet doesn't turn into a hot mud pit with no fresh food and no polar bears or whatever."

I'm shocked. I say I understand, but I don't, at least not entirely. I don't get to the part where I beg her to go see Tyler Anderson, The East Coast Medium, with me this weekend. My texts from last night are just the kick-off of the campaign I'd put together to convince her to go with me to the city this weekend. The texts were just to let her know, but I hadn't actually begged yet. There's no way she's going. That's evident. I am on my own. I need to go now more than ever. I need some guidance. I need to know what to do next. I know I have to save the planet, but I don't know how. Suddenly, she stands up and grabs her heavy bag.

"'I've got to go, SAM. I need to talk to Mr. Henry before Visual Arts. I took some pictures last weekend that I want him to help me with." She takes a few steps and then turns around. Her perfectly curled hair bounces as she turns.

"Simone, I trust you. I believe you. You know I know the environment is messed up. It basically killed my mom. I just, I don't know, I just, I just can't right now. I can't do what you need me to do even though I don't really know what you want from me. But I'm here for you. You know that, right? I'm sorry. I gotta go. I'll see you after school. My dad is picking me up. Ride home with me and I'll ask him to take us to Nathan's. I saw on Insta this morning that they have Pumpkin Pie Ice Cream starting today. I know you love it." She turns back around and walks away. Her curls moving carefully with her.

That night after I spend TWO HOURS on my pre-cal homework, I get my phone out and start scheming. I need to get to Tyler Anderson, The East Coast Medium *this* weekend. I don't care what anyone says. What I felt and saw in my dream is real. I need help figuring out what to do about the dream. What is coming? What help can the universe give me? Who can give me answers I can't find in the physical world? I know I have to do something, but what? I need direction. I need supernatural guidance. I need divine intervention.

I can't just sit by and let another catastrophe happen without trying to intervene. I've learned my lesson. I'll never make the mistake of being silent ever again. Never. I have a voice. I'm going to use it. Not the most normal thing that I can do right now, but psychic duty calls. I'm sure it seems selfish, but not only did Mrs. Carpenter die, I almost died. I realize that is my own fault. I am the one who downed the pills. I'm the one who was so depressed and in so much pain that I tried to numb everything. That's how devastating the guilt is. That's how heavy the weight of being different can fee sometimes. Guilt is a dragon, a cancer, a covering, a weight, a distraction, a tape-worm eating me alive from the inside. My Guilt Dragon has been with me since as early as I can remember. My earliest childhood memories aren't of merry-go-rounds and princess-themed birthday parties. They are of guilt and shame and confusion and helplessness. Headaches. Throwing up near the cubbies and on my nap mat.

CHAPTER TWO

Thursday, August 29

By Thursday, I have most of a plan in place. I'm just missing one thing. I don't bring it up with Connelly again; she makes it clear she is out. I don't want to make her mad again. After our Nathan's Dairy Bar date with Mr. Carpenter, we fall back into our regular rhythm, and I leave it at that. I don't ask her again about Tyler Anderson, The East Coast Medium, or mention my latest dream anymore. She doesn't ask either, though. It feels weird to have something between us. Like a little ghost. You can't really see it, but you can feel it. When I realize Connelly isn't going with me, I go online and buy one of the few remaining tickets to see Tyler Anderson, The East Coast Medium, live in and person at the National Sixth Sense Conference. I feel a familiar electric energy run through my body as I confirm my purchase. I give the rabbit's foot in my pocket three quick taps.

If I could, I would spend all three days at the conference learning as much as I can about premonitions, precognitive dreams, fortune telling, and all of those amazingly cool and kooky things. If you're going to be a weirdo, you might as well know a lot about it. With my gifts, It's hard to fit in with the

Muggles, but I also don't want to take my powers for granted. Part of the responsibility of being psychic is knowing about your power. I won't be holding a workshop in the cafeteria for my classmates on how to tap into your extrasensory perceptions, but I can at least know what's up with my own. The more I know, the more I hope to be able to use my powers for good. I need to learn more so that I can tame my body's reactions to the energy, like the headaches and the anxiety. Those have got to go.

The conference is Friday, Saturday, and Sunday. No way can I miss school on Friday though, and Tyler Anderson, The East Coast Medium's session is on Saturday. I make my plans around his 5:00 PM reading. I can't be gone all day either; my parents will ask too many questions. I figure I can leave around noon and get to the city in time to meet some of the other conference vendors and still get to my seat in time to not miss a minute of Tyler Anderson, The East Coast Medium. I'll take the train into Union Station and then walk to the Convention Center. I'll have time to get something quick to eat at Union Kitchen Grocery. My fave. My mouth waters at the thought of a big thick slab of a MilkCult Vanilla Chocolate Chip ice cream sandwich. Give me all the ice cream.

As for what I'll tell my parents, I don't know yet. It's not that they won't let me go to the city, but they won't let me go alone. Meaning, my plan isn't complete yet. I just need one more thing: a partner in crime. It's not like I don't have other friends besides Connelly, I do. Honestly, I do. I swear. It's just hard to have a lot of friends when you have a best friend like Connelly. You don't need many more people in your life. She is so much love and goodness wrapped into one human. That aside, the reason I need to go to D.C. is critical and kind, and let's face it, peculiar. It's not a trip to the zoo or the Smithsonian. I can't just tell any ol' body the details of my mission. I have one option, but it's complicated.

Khalil. Khalil is Connelly's cousin. His mom is, *was*, Mrs. Carpenter's sister. Khalil lives in our neighborhood, but goes to All Saints, the private high school close by. Khalil has been crushing on me since the days of pre-school and Nick Jr. He is so annoying. Mostly he's annoying because, well, he's a 15 year old boy. All he cares about is wrestling. That's why he goes to All Saints; they have the best wrestling team in the Mid Atlantic. It's all he ever talks about or thinks about or does anything about. Well, except me. He thinks about me a lot too. He texts me every single day. He sends me new music he thinks I'll like and will expand my musical horizons into the modern era. He doesn't get my commitment to the Dead. Most of the music he sends are love songs, and I pretend not to like them. Sometimes I do though, just a little. But, what Khalil has working in his favor is that he listens to every word I say and believes me too. He takes my dreams and me seriously. Honestly, he's a really good friend. I should give him more credit. He always remembers my birthday and brings Cherry Garcia little treats. I should be nicer to him now that I really think about it.

When we were in sixth grade, I dreamed that he broke his arm during the final match of the season. Back then, I sometimes used my powers for evil instead of good. Before his match, I told him about the dream, and then I told him to break an arm. Like instead of break a leg, which is what you're supposed to tell actors before a show. Except, he did actually break his arm. I mean, I knew he was going to, but I didn't have to be so mean about it. To this day, I feel bad about saying that to him. Also, Connelly told him about the dream I had about her mom, his aunt. She said she needed someone to talk to about everything that was happening. I don't know if he is mad at me about it or not. He's never said anything to me about it one way or another. It's actually quite kind of him to give me that space. Either way, ever since the sixth grade, he wants to know about all of my dreams. He's a believer. I should probably take Dr. A's advice and talk to him about Mrs. Carpenter. He already knows anyways. He also knows enough about me that I don't have to over explain my mission and why I need to go see Tyler Evans, the East Coast Medium. He will be supportive and not act like I'm a freak show.

The complicated thing is that I don't want to lead him on. No matter what, Khalil is my friend and he's Connelly's cousin. I don't want to hurt him. I'm pretty sure he thinks I'm the love of his life. I can assure you, I am not. This time though, he's my only option. I know he'll go with me and will also understand why I need to go. My mom and dad love Khalil. As long as he goes with me, they will say yes. He'll also wait for me and not care (too much) that I don't have a ticket for him. Maybe he can watch the livestream on his phone while I'm inside, or maybe he will practice his wrestling moves or whatever at Urban Athletic Club. That is actually something that he would do. He's really obsessed with wrestling. I text Khalil.

u free sat?

depends

jk

always for you

need ur help

sup

trip 2 dc

cool time?

meet me @ the station @ 12:15

xoxo

am i right?

or am i right

gross

stop

for real

bye

thx

conn coming?

nah ur uncle won't let her

k

later

yw

Sweet. Done deal. I call my mom and "ask" her if I can go. She says yes, but I have to be back by ten, my regular stupid baby curfew. Now I wait. Impatiently. Very impatiently.

CHAPTER THREE

Friday, August 30

On Fridays, I have therapy with Dr. Ambrossini. I love therapy. You can add that to my weirdo factor. I started going last year after my overdose. Obviously, I was really upset by the dream *and then* her diagnosis *and then* her death *and then* the relentless attacks of the Guilt Dragon. The only way I got out of the hospital was to schedule ongoing, weekly therapy with a physiatrist specializing in grief and depression. I'd been working with Dr. A off and on, so it made sense to pick up with her more frequently. Dr. A helps me work through the guilt and other confusing emotions. She also helps me process my other dreams and deal with my standard issue anxiety. She's got her hands full.

Dr. A listens to me and talks me through anything I have on my mind. Today, I'm telling her about my latest dream, a Big One. The End of the World as we Know it One. The Death to all Beings One. Her office is near my school, and my mom and dad are both working this afternoon, so I walk over by myself. I haven't talked to my parents about my dream yet. They support me and trust me, but also hate that I get really upset and stressed out by the dreams. They also worry about the anxiety

I feel knowing that my dreams come true. Plus after my pills incident last year, they are mad sensitive to the slightest change in my mood, feelings, demeanor, slang, expressions, clothing, songs, and on and on and on.

Parents on high alert status. I feel bad about that and don't want to incite a parent riot unless I have to. I want to talk to Dr. A about my dream first. She'll help me gather my thoughts and get logical rather than just straight up emotional. I also want to go the Sixth Sense Conference to see Tyler Anderson, The East Coast Medium, before I talk to my parents. I need direction from all sources including them. I just need a plan, and I want it to seem like I'm in control. If I'm losing it, then they are definitely going to freak out. A freak out could include admitting me to the psych ward again, and I just can't do that again. Never. They will be upset if I'm upset. I don't want anyone else to be any more upset than necessary. I need to get organized. Get in formation. #Beyoncé

Dr. A bounds out of her office like a Labrador puppy that's been crated for way too long. She appears in the waiting room to greet me. She's always bouncing a little bit. She's tall like me and broad shouldered with soft, fluffy curves everywhere else. Some days I just want to sit in her lap and snuggle her. To be clear, I'm not a snuggler. Her hair is platinum blonde. Like really, really for real blonde. For some reason this is sort of funny to me. Her face is wide and just a tiny bit doughy. It's all big smiles and big frowns depending on the conversation. She probably can't play poker. She wears the same thing every Friday. Skinny jeans that are very skinny at the bottom and then widen as they follow her body. She wears flowy Bohemian tops in tropical colors. No white. No black. No gray. No brown. Colors. Even though she already towers over most of her patients, she wears chunky platforms or tall wedges. A little bit of her ivory skin always sticks out in the space between her jeans and her shoes.

For some reason, I always end up staring at it. Her skin is nearly translucent. Like worn out teeth. She wears stacks of bangles and bracelets of every shape and size on each wrist. Threaded friendship bracelets. Copper cuffs. Silver charms. She makes a lot of noise when she talks with her hands, which is quite a lot. She's everything you'd imagine a therapist who is cool with people like me to be, except the hair. That part is surprising.

I don't know why, but she really likes me or at least acts like she does. She brings me back to her office. I love it so much. It's a miniature rectangle of a space, more like a big utility closet and less like a real office. Everything is white. Everything. She has a white two-seater love seat with way too many white pillows arranged artistically on it. They are all different shapes and sizes. They come in so many textures: bumpy, smooth, silky, coarse, velvety, lacy, and crocheted. On the white walls in white wooden frames, she has white paintings. They are completely white but have all sorts of textures. The white paint makes ridges, sculpted waves, and scalloped edges. I want to feel them. I want to touch each little bump and spike. She sits on the end of a small white, square shaped chair, and hands me a white chenille blanket. It's my favorite thing in the office. The only colorful things in the whole room are the beautiful paper birds hanging from the ceiling. They come in every color of the rainbow. They hang at different heights. Some high. Some low. The ones in the middle seem to want to be the highest or the lowest, but there they are stuck in between. When the vent blows, the birds sway and dance a little. I feel so much calmer when I visit Dr. Ambrossini. She makes it easy to sit, talk, and feel better.

I plop down on the white loveseat and tuck my long legs beneath me. I position myself so that I can see the paper birds as I talk. Before Dr. A can even ask me what's on my mind, I start right in.

"Dr. A, it happened again." I'm a little breathless. "A Big One. I'm scared. I've been trying to hold it together all week and I'm dying inside. I'm terrified. I feel sick. I couldn't wait to get here today. I've been needing to talk to you so badly." My throat tightens. My ~~voice catches in my throat~~. I reach for a sip of water. My feelings coat my throat like motor oil. She sucks her breath in smoothly and nods encouragingly for me to go on.

The dream tumbles out of me. I tell her about the world of desolation, hunger, and chaos. I describe the rations, the fish-less seas, and the bird-less skies. I tell her about the unforgiving heat and the standing water, thick as wells of ink. I explain that everyone is forced to move to cities and live together, miserable, in neglected, overcrowded buildings. Everyone is angry, hungry, thirsty, and disappointed. I tell her about the decimation of Miami and my beloved New Orleans. They are just gone. They fell right into the ocean. My grandparents' home on the bayou is no more. No more shrimp. No more crawdads. No more walks through the French Quarter. No more beignets from Café du Monde. I stop for a minute to catch my breath and collect my thoughts. Dr. Ambrossini looks at me intently and then asks, "Simone, what are you going to do?"

She knows me well, and she believes me. Relief splashes over me like a sprinkler's mist on a steamy Virginia day. My throat closes up quickly I react to Dr. A's kindness. It's hard to swallow. Tenth grade Simone cries way more than ninth grade Simone. It makes it hard to answer her. "I don't know yet," I croak.

"Ok, that's fine, Simone. You don't have to have all the answers. You're not in this alone. You have help. Let's talk it out. Let me make sure I understand how you are feeling. You've had a dream that you think is going to come true. You're basing this on your past experiences that have proven true. In the dream, you see the future of the earth if we don't take climate change seriously. At this point, you believe you need to do something with this information, but you aren't sure what to do yet. Does that sound like what you told me, Simone?" I nod. I love this woman.

"Simone, this is very serious based on your history of mental health. We all know the toll that the last dream had on you. There are major repercussions on your health when you have one of these major precognitive dreams. I can't let that happen again. You might have a mission, but I have one too." She smiles at me to assure me she's on my side.

I nod. I know she's right. This is tricky. I have to do something. I don't know what I can do that will make a difference and also protect myself at the same time. That seems like an impossible task. I can't make myself sick again. I know that. I can't spend another year of my life fighting the Guilt Dragon, being depressed, and living afraid.

"Simone, I'm going to do my best to help you in every way that I can. I am here to help you. I'm not going to let you fall. This is going to be a lot of work for both of us, but I know we are up for the challenge. We're a team. A dream team!" She laughs at her own corny joke. I manage a laugh at her laughing. "I'm going to hold you accountable for handling your mental health. I won't accept excuses or slackness. Your well-being, right now, on this earth is all that we have today. It's my number one concern. Is that okay with you?" I nod. I know she's right. I need her, but I also need to do what I need to do. I just need to know what that is.

"Okay, good. First thing's first, my dear Simone. Are you taking your medication? You have to take it every single day. You know that. It's not an option." I nod again. Less enthusiastically, but it's a yes nonetheless. "Great. Let's brainstorm. What do you know about climate change today, Simone?"

"Well, my mom watches the news every morning, so I see some things that are going on in the world. You know, how like, President Robinson will veto a bill, or whatever, and then the news will say that if she had approved it, then it would really help the environment a lot. Or, like, I know about recycling and how the earth is getting warmer. I think the heat is what causes more hurricanes and tornadoes and extreme temperatures and things like that. I think. I'm not sure."

"Yes, that's a good summary of what most people commonly know. You're paying attention, Simone. That's great. I'm proud of you for taking an interest in the world around you. How could you learn more about the climate crisis, Simone?"

"Umm, I guess I could like do some research on the internet. That's easy. Maybe watch some documentaries and things like that."

"Sure. All great ideas, Simone. What else?" Dr. A is calm and watches me closely.

"Oh, ok. Um, I could read a book, I guess. Maybe I could talk to someone who knows more about stuff like this than I do, which is probably anyone actually."

Dr. A nods and says, "Yes, Simone, those are all fantastic. So, I'm hearing you say that you will do some research on the internet, check out some other resources such as books and movies. Great! When you're on the internet, just make sure that you are using reliable, unbiased sources. That's a good start. Getting the facts will help ground you, and you'll feel less overwhelmed if you have data. That data can then help you to come up with your plan. I know you want to do something. I understand why you have to do something. I'd rather you take action than not, all things considered. Taking action will keep you from getting depressed. I think that's a fair assessment. Let's keep brainstorming. Who do you know that you could talk to?" I think about it for a second and then it hits me like an angry boxer's left hook.

"I know who I can talk to!" I can't believe I didn't think about this before. Connelly's dad is like a huge environmental science guy. He's like a professor or something like that. He knows everything about the environment." In my excitement, I forget about how this might seem to Connelly or even to Mr. Carpenter. He's always been a super science guy, but maybe he's not that into it now because of what happened with Mrs. Carpenter. I haven't really been paying that much attention to really know. I know he's my best shot though. I have to take the chance. I'm thinking hard about this possible conflict of interest.

"Simone, what are you thinking about? You went radio silent."

I don't want to get into my concern about sharing all of this or certain parts of it with Mr. Carpenter and Connelly because, well, honestly, I don't want Dr. A to tell me not to talk to him about it. She might be afraid that it will trigger me. But he's the only person I know that has enough of the information that I need.

"Nothing, nothing. I'm good, Dr. A. Thank you. That was helpful. I know what to do. I'm going over to Connelly's tonight for French FRYday. Mr. Carpenter makes us black bean burgers and French fries every Friday. He loves it and I'm learning to like, not love, black bean burgers, I guess."

We talk about a few other things. She asks me more questions about school, and how I've been feeling since we last talked. She reminds to do my breathing exercises and to make sure I journal or talk to my parents or Connelly if I get anxious between sessions. She reinforces my meds one more time just in case I didn't hear her earlier. She asks me about any crushes, dates, or love interests that I might have. My answer is always a hard no. She must not remember what 15-year-old boys are like. I consider telling her about Khalil and our trip to D.C. to see Tyler Anderson, The East Coast Medium, at the Sixth Sense conference, but it seems like a can of worms that I don't want to open. I stick with my hard no and then we finish up with a hug. She gives the best hugs. I feel better. I feel like I have the first steps of a plan.

I go over to Connelly's once she gets home from work. She's the front desk girl at a salon near her house. She's waiting on the front porch for me. I can see her eyelashes from the sidewalk. Probably they can be seen from space. She's been known to come back from the salon with various experiments from time to time. When ombre was a big thing, she was always coming home with some sort of version of a blonde ombre experiment. It always looked the same to me, but she assured me they were all very different. I just nod and agree.

"Conn-Woman, you look like you have giant spiders attached to your eyelids. Are you okay? Can you even see through those things?" I'm laughing. It feels good to laugh with her or at her in this case. I can't believe she has those attached to her face. She laughs too and admits that her eyelids feel like they have Legos attached to them. She hopes she can make it through the Netflix binge we have planned. Her mom loved the *Babysitters Club* books when she was young, and Netflix made them into a TV series. I wouldn't choose them myself, but I'd do anything to make Connelly feel better about missing her mom. It's the least I can do. Let's be honest. Guilt Dragon. Claw. Hiss. Growl. Attack.

"You're right. I'm going upstairs to take these dumb things off. I don't want to miss a minute of Claudia and Kristy's babysitting crisis of the week!" Her enthusiasm is almost contagious. She tries to wink at me but it doesn't go well with the sweep of eyelashes glued to her face. They are stuck and she has a hard time getting her eye un-blinked. Connelly traipses upstairs to extricate her eyelashes and get her sight back. I hear Mr. Carpenter calls out a greeting, and I walk to the kitchen to say hello. He stands mashing his bean burgers together as he balances on one foot in tree pose. He looks up at me, sheepish, and grins a hello.

"Simone! How's it hanging, kiddo? Working on my balance." He points his chin to his standing leg to indicate his effort. I give him the thumbs up because I don't know what else to do. "You'll be happy to know that I'm not only working on my balance, but I'm also working on perfecting my world famous black bean burger recipe. In honor of your taste buds, I've added a secret ingredient to the mix."

"I hope it's beef," I say dryly. He barks out a laugh and actually slaps his knee. He ends up spreading mashed beans on his tan khakis. They don't need an extra stain; they already look like they've been recycled for a hundred years. "Ha, ha, kiddo. Nope. Nada. No beef at Casa Carpenter. You know that. I'll call you girls down when the best black bean burgers of your life are ready." I shrug and nod, but then pause. Now's as good a time as ever.

"Hey, Mr. Carpenter, can I ask you something first?" He stops his mashing and looks at me with a curious glance.

"Sure, heck-ya, kiddo. What's on your mind?"

Nervous, I clear my throat. There's no way I'm mentioning the dream. I just need to know what to do to save the planet. Simple as that. How hard can that be? Be normal. "So, I, um, I'm wondering about, you know, the environment. I mean, like, what can someone like me do about it....besides not eat beef."

"Oh, geez, kid. You had me worried. You look so darn serious. It's a hard answer and an easy answer. There's a lot that you can do to personally limit your carbon footprint. Like eating less beef, you're right about that. Also, you can travel by walking or riding your bike. You can buy fewer material things like clothes and shoes. You can eat a plant-based diet. You can buy responsibly when you do really need something. You can research where goods come from and buy local, sustainable goods. You probably know all those things though, don't you, Simone?"

"Uh, yeah, I guess. I mean I still eat bacon and steaks though." I also look down at my new Vans and feel a pang of remorse. The Guilt Dragon says hello. I probably didn't *need* new shoes for back to school.

"Ha, yes, of course you do. I know it's hard at first. I missed filet mignon for a decade before I forgot about it for good."

Talk about depressing. "Oh, ok. I'll try and do better. More salads and tofu or whatever, I guess. But, like, is that all?"

"Well, no we are always learning and adding to the list of what each person can do differently to restore the Earth, but what we really need is systemic change to reverse the course we are on and make a meaningful long-term impact. We need the government to step up. President Robinson's administration has done nothing to address the pollution that is causing so many problems; in fact, she has done things to make it worse. She's withdrawn us from one of the most important global climate initiatives, and then she deletes the mention of climate change from governmental science updates. She's even blocked congressional testimony on climate related issues. She's repealed some of the Environmental Protection Agency's most important Earth saving plans. She's turned back the clock on many of the environmental standards that have been in place for some time now. She's de-regulating the wrong industries, quite frankly. We can't wait another four years for another president and party to take on climate change. She's up for re-election and has already begun campaigning. If she's paying attention to anything at all, then she has to see that both parties are ready to face climate change. As a bi-partisan candidate, she's in the perfect position to appeal to both sides as long as she gets on the right side of history. It's an important issue for this election. The polls are showing that we are at a critical mass of belief in the climate crisis and that most voting citizens are demanding climate crisis action immediately."

"Mr. Carpenter," I interrupt. I can tell he is about to go on a very long and detailed rant, and I'm already completely overwhelmed. I barely understand any of what he is saying especially when it comes to what I can do about the climate crisis. What I can do about my dream. How can I get him to narrow it down so I know where to start?

"What's the most important thing that needs to happen to stop the climate crisis?" I ask him directly.

"Ah, yes. Good question. It can be overwhelming, huh?" He accurately reads the expression on my face. "Well, kiddo, that would be up to President Robinson and convincing her of the science of the climate crisis. She doesn't believe in the work that my colleagues and I have presented to her cabinet. I'm not sure what is happening between our presentations to them and what they actually tell her about our research. The facts, the science. Without her support of the scientific data, we will not be able to stop the climate crisis before it is too late. Today, we have all the technology that we need to stop, reverse, and restore the planet, but we are running out of time. Now is the time. Not four years from now. We can't waste any more time. We can't wait for another President. We have to have her on our side. She's the tipping point."

His voice rises sharply when he speaks. The passion, commitment, and conviction strong and condemning as he lays out what needs to be done. At the end of his long-winded answer, his voice drops. Some of us already ran out of time. Mrs. Carpenter ran out of time. Oh shit. I knew this would happen. I tried so hard to be nonchalant and not upset him. I clearly fail him again. The room is quiet for a second, and then I hear Connelly calling for me. I thank Mr. Carpenter for the chat and slink to the staircase. I hate that I've upset him.

For the rest of the evening, I try to focus on Logan and Mary Anne's latest dating spat. Reason 1,007 that I am not down for a "love interest" as Dr. A calls it. I'm distracted by Mr. Carpenter's answer. How the hell am I supposed to get the President to believe in science? Didn't she go to school and college? Isn't she in charge of the free world? Seriously? I think about it all night. I sleep fitfully in Connelly's room even though I'm cozy next to her. Oddly enough, I hope for another dream. Not a Big One but one that will give me direction. I feel lost but committed. Confused but determined.

CHAPTER FOUR

Saturday, August 31

O n Saturday, I wake up with a start. No dream. Maybe that's a good thing. Maybe just one Big One is enough for right now. I am anxious to get home and organize my conference supplies. I have a stack of books to get signed. I still have to pack my journal and gel pens for notetaking. There's no way I can leave Connelly's house before breakfast though. Second to French FRYday, Saturday morning pancakes are another Carpenter-Marker tradition. This Saturday it's blackberry buckwheat. They are surprisingly delicious, and I eat mine with reckless abandon. Thankfully, Connelly has to work at ten, so after breakfast, her dad and I walk her to the salon. Afterwards, I run the rest of the way home to get ready. My phone buzzes in my hand. I glance down.

c u at 12:15

try not to fall n luv w me

I roll my eyes, but am reassured. I hadn't texted him since Thursday. I've been ignoring his songs.

k thx

i wont unless u bring ice cream then maybe

I tap the little green arrow. Damnit. That's way too much. I'm trying to balance friendly with inviting but not too inviting. I don't want to lead him on. Why did I send that? I'm so awkward. That was weird. I do love ice cream though, so maybe all is not lost. Silver linings and all that.

At 12:15 on the money, Khalil walks up the station holding a pint of Moorenko's Wild Blueberry. It's not my favorite flavor of all time, but he tries hard. I don't say anything; I spoon cold sweetness into my mouth instead. We wait quietly for the train. Khalil looks at me intently but also says nothing. When we settle in our seats, he finally asks me what's going on. I still have a lot of ice cream to eat, and I take my time between icy bites to bring him up to speed. The comfort of the ice cream somehow makes it easier to bare my soul. I start at the beginning with Mrs. Carpenter since technically he already knows about her anyways, and not just from me. I recount it all. The dream. The devastation. The Guilt Dragon. The fact that I have no idea what I should do about this, but that I have no doubt that I need to do something. I can't sit back and sit still. He nods a lot. He doesn't interrupt. He's a good listener, actually. When I get to the details of today, he isn't thrilled that he is going to have to wait for me while I go to see Tyler Anderson, The East Coast Medium, on my own, but he doesn't complain too much. I'm telling you, for whatever reason, the boy loves me. I should be kinder to him, really.

Even though I just housed down an excessive amount of ice cream, I can't resist hitting up Union Kitchen Grocery before going inside the Convention Center. We share a small pizza and one of the ice cream sandwiches that I can't get out of my head. I talk excitedly about the conference; Khalil listens closely. I can't help but notice that we get fewer stares when we are in D.C. versus when are in Longview. Apparently, suburbia is still not used to seeing a peach-skinned person and a nutmeg-skinned person eating a freaking meal together. I still love the look on people's face when they learn Connelly and Khalil are cousins.

Khalil's mom and Connelly's mom are, were, both white, and Khalil's dad is black. Khalil talks about how hard it is to figure out where he feels most comfortable. It's easier at his school than at mine because at his school there are so few non-white kids that is forces everyone to co-mingle. At my school, it's harder to move between groups. I'm saddened when I walk into the cafeteria and see that there are tables white kids, tables of black kids, and tables of brown kids. Not a lot of tables of more than one shade.

At All Saints where Khalil goes to school, he is the only student who is biracial. There is one other student, Habib, who is black and an exchange student from Nigeria. He's a math genius, and Khalil, even though he's really smart, he's not the most studious guy. It's hard for him to sit still and just read to read. He likes to move. Everyone assumes that Khalil and Habib should automatically be friends because they look similar, but Khalil said they aren't vibing yet. My guess is Habib isn't into wrestling and that narrows down Khalil's circle considerably. There are twin girls who are African American. All Khalil ever says about them is that they are "dope as hell." I don't get the impression that they give him the time of day, or I imagine he'd have a lot more to say about them. Realizing my mind is wandering all over the place, I bring it back into focus. Dr. A has been working with me on this. I ask Khalil how school is going, and his answer is about wrestling. Per usual. He gets so excited about it though. It's kind of cute. He tells me all about his training and the pre-season exhibition that he's going to be in. He talks about his coach and his teammates as if they are preparing to go off to war. Even though he's just a sophomore, he's still a co-captain. That's how much he loves it, he wants to lead it. It's hard not to admire his passion and talent.

By the time we finish eating, it's nearly 2:45. I am dying to get inside the Convention Center. Reluctantly, Khalil leaves me at the Grande Lobby doors. He says he will be back at 6:15 to get me. I have no idea what he's going to do, and I'm not his babysitter, so I wave him off and all but skip into the building. This is my chance to get what I need to **do** something about my dream. Sixth Sense Conference people can see through the immediate bullshit of today and see clearly into the future. They know what's coming and they can tell me what to do. I need my people, odd as we may be, we at least have each other.

I can barely contain myself. I want to run up and down the rows and rows of vendors. It smells like incense, patchouli, and lavender. These are my people. Here I feel like I fit in. I feel understood and not judged. I feel celebrated and not like a big freak. What makes me abnormal, feels normal here. Here I blend right in. No NORMAL mantra needed. There are booths and booths of palmists, fortune tellers, astrologists, healers, energy readers, chromotherapists, crystal enthusiasts, psychics, homeopaths, reflexologists, channelists, ghost hunters, numerologists, and last but not least mediums. My favorite. I take my time going to each booth and feeling the energy of each of the vendors. I seek out the authors of the books I brought with me to get signed. I'm straight up giddy. I like being here with a community of people who are probably weirder than me. I mean unique, more unique than me. And not crazy. I won't say crazy today. That's for your Dr. A. I spend extra time at a medium perched on the last row near the entrance to the meeting room where I'm seeing Tyler Anderson, The East Coast Medium. She draws me in with her round, searching, mahogany eyes and open posture.

"Hi," I say.

"You lookin' for something specific, ain't you, Queen Canary?" She draws out the word Queen. Her deep Southern accent cradling my cherished nickname. My jaw drops. I consciously pick it up and close my mouth. Then I open it again. I stammer, "What did you call me?"

"Queen Canary. That's yo name, aint it?" She grins at me knowingly. How do adults know how to grin knowingly?

"Well, yeah, I mean, yes it is, but only my mom and dad call me that and only when I'm stressed out and stuff."

"You seem a little stressed to me, darlin' Queen. I'm gettin' very powerful energy from you right now."

"I'm not. I mean, I kinda am. Yeah, I'm here for an important reason. The most important reason, really. So also I'm excited. Actually, I'm really, really excited. I'm going to see Tyler Anderson, The East Coast Medium. I have to get a reading from him. I have to. Like I said, it's really important."

"You do, do ya? And why's that, darlin'?"

I think she should probably already know since she's a medium and all. Also, she already freaked me out by knowing my very secret nickname. I tilt my head and frown at her just a little to show my slight distrust. I suddenly feel snarky. "You don't already know?"

She looks back at me with a calm expression and soothing voice. She says plainly, "Ya already have everything ya need to do what ya need to do." Ugh. My instinct is wrong. I shouldn't have stopped here after all. She may know my name, but she doesn't know anything else about me and what I need. She has no idea what I'm trying to do here. I have a planet to save. Images of tan pucks of freeze-dried food clutter my mind. I feel the loss of my grandparents' house and hometown like a handful of missing puzzle pieces. I see the dull steely sky. No golden sun, but blazing hot. It's almost time for the doors to open for my session with Tyler Anderson, The East Coast Medium and I am not going to miss a minute of it because of this uncanny kook. I thank her for her vague advice and make my way to the ballroom.

I can't believe other people made it to the doors before me. Damnit. Those early birds must have some serious issues if they beat *me* to the punch. I am about fifty people back. I can still get a front row seat, probably even in the middle section. It will just take a little creative maneuvering. I can see through the doors, and the ballroom is enormous. I scurry through the people with the crazy, mad issues. I may or may not heavily nudge a few old people as I elbow my through the crowd. I do it! I land a first row seat, slightly to the left of center. There's still 20 mins before the reading begins. I settle in and organize my note-book and pens. I pick up my phone and text Khalil.

im in

cool

im watching

watching what creeper

the livestream troll

salty bruh

I'm impressed he's watching the livestream. Not too many dudes would do that. I power my phone down. I'm not going to miss a thing. The next 15 minutes are the longest of my life. I pass the time by watching people find their seats. It's an eclectic group of people for sure. All ages, all sizes, all races. One lady has what looks like a colorful pigeon perching on her shoulder. They are pouring in and scrambling for a good seat. They should've gotten here earlier if I do say so myself.

The lights start to flicker and upbeat house music booms through the giant speakers situated throughout the ballroom. There must be 5,000 people in the room, and they are all on their feet. I'm jumping and screaming louder than anyone. I briefly wonder how the pigeon is handling this, but I keep bouncing up and down. Everyone is clapping and high-fiving. It's basically the Super Bowl of the pseudoscience community. I'm going to be hoarse tomorrow. Several songs play and the en-ergy gets higher and heavier, like it is a living breathing being in the room with us. The room goes pitch black and a drumroll rumbles through the ballroom. Suddenly the lights pop on, and Tyler Anderson, The East Coast Medium rises up from a platform beneath the floor. When he's flush with the stage, a huge smile spreads across his face and he welcomes us to the reading. He begins by telling us, his adoring fans, about himself but we already know everything about him. He says that sometimes, he'll have messages for us from the universe (which is what I'm hoping for), and sometimes he'll have messages for us from someone that has died and been promoted to the other side. He tells us the session will be one hour long and he'll get to as many of us who have messages waiting as he can. I am worried and hopeful that he might go past an hour, but I can't stay if he does. The last train to Longview leaves Union Station at 6:49 PM. Khalil will be waiting outside at 6:15.

He begins the reading with a message for an ancient lady SITTING NEAR THE BACK. This seems unfair. She probably didn't even get here early. It is sad though. Her son died from a drug overdose, opioids probably. Parents shouldn't outlive their children. He was in his forties when he passed over. He wants her to know he's sorry and he's at peace now. He also wants her to stop going to the cemetery every day. He tells her he's not there. When Tyler Anderson, The East Coast Medium does a reading, it seems like he turns into a different person. He seems to be the person that he's receiving the message from. It's super weird; I love it. When he talks to the old lady's son, he develops an accent hailing from Alabama. His words slow way down and drip like honey on a fluffy biscuit.

He then moves on to another couple SITTING IN THE MIDDLE of the room, again they didn't even get here early. He has a message from the universe for this couple. He tells them to keep trying. That's all he says, and they both burst into tears and grab each other's' arms and shoulders as if they are going to float away if they don't hold on tight. That is enough for them. Tyler Anderson, The East Coast Medium moves on to the left side of the room. WHY ISN'T HE AT THE FRONT OF THE ROOM WHERE THE EARLY BIRDS ARE? HIS SUPERFANS ARE IN THE FRONT ROW. HELLO! A middle-age man gets a message from his sister.

She died two years ago in a drunk driving accident. She says not to worry about her anymore. She's with their favorite old dog from their childhood, Buddy (of course). She tells him that their dad is alive and lives in San Francisco. His name is Jose Alberto Lopez. She tells him to go find him. Just show up on the doorstep. Alberto is waiting for him. He has been for a long time. The whole room sniffles at the same time at this one.

Tyler Anderson, The East Coast Medium moves around the left side of the room sharing a few one-liners from the universe to a few lucky people. One guy, a little older than me, learns he's going to get a scholarship and to stop worrying and just enjoy high school. Damn. Must be nice. One man about my dad's age finds out he's going to get the job he's always wanted. He just needs to quit the one he's got and take a chance. I don't know that I've ever seen anyone look happier than that dude. A little girl, about ten maybe, gets a message that she's going to get adopted. She just has to be patient and stop stealing from her foster parents. She looks extremely guilty (I feel you kid), then cries violently, then smiles ecstatically in a matter of about fifteen seconds. Little kids are great.

He moves to the right side of the room. I'm actually dying now. It's 5:45. The messages take longer to download, receive, and share than you think. There is a set of twins. My age. Gorgeous. He tells one to give him a chance. He tells the other embrace her truth with courage. To stand tall in who she really is. The twins lock eyes and nod their long matching braids at each other. The beads at the ends tinkling together and sounding like a tiny, perfect wind chime. They giggle; the kind of laugh that I wish I had, but I have more of a snort. Like a grumbling pig. They sound more like human sized fairies. He does a reading for a lady who is younger than my mom, maybe like 30 or so with bright red hair springing off her head like a mess of coils. She is already crying before Tyler Anderson, The East Coast Medium even gets to her. He tells her that her mother who died of cancer is so proud of her. She doesn't need to do anything or become anything more than she is. The mother loves the woman fully and completely. The message for the red-haired lady is to rest and relax and enjoy life.

Then he asks who else is there for a message from someone who has recently died of cancer. Damnit. That's not me either and we are running out of time. There are only a few minutes left. I bite my bottom lip impatiently. Tyler Anderson, The East Coast Medium is finally walking towards the front of the room, but he's not looking for me. I am there for a message from the universe. Who would know better how to get the President to believe in science and save the earth than the actual universe itself? I wish whomever is supposed to get this message would hurry up and receive it so that I can have a turn. I'm considering just raising my hand and asking for a reading if he doesn't offer me a message. I don't know if it works like that. No one else has asked for a message. As I debate with myself what my next move is, I lose track of him. Suddenly he's standing at the end of my row.

"The message is for someone in this area," he waves his hand to indicate the row of chairs I'm in. I look up and down the row, impatient for someone to claim the message so we can move on. "I'm getting a message for a young person." He pauses and closes his eyes. "A young person who has a big mission. An important mission." Oh, shit. I have the most important mission. But who would have a message for me? Someone who died of cancer? Wait. I've been so focused on a message from the universe I never considered another option. Could it be Mrs. Carpenter? Holy shit. Why am I just thinking about this now? I swallow hard and clear my throat. I raise my hand.

"Aha! I knew it," he says with excitement. He walks confidently to my chair and places a hand on my shoulder. "I'm getting a message from someone who was close to you. She wants you to forgive yourself."

I'm crying...again. It's a deep, gentle cry. A therapeutic

one. The tears are warm, salty, instant, and cleansing. They feel good on my face. I need this message after all. A sense of peace and clarity that I haven't felt in a long time fills me up. I feel lighter. He keeps going though. "She says the answer is true love. The answer is always true love." I can hear Mrs. Carpenter in the way he says the words without question. Her teacher voice, direct and frank with authority. The kind of voice you don't ignore. You take notes and know it's true. He begins to walk away, satisfied and triumphant, but I'm not ready for him to be finished. I got a message I needed, but not the answer I came for. What's love got to do with anything?

"Wait," I half shout. "But, what about President Robinson? How will I get her to change her mind? How will she believe the science?" My voice is desperate and shrill. He of course has no idea what I'm talking about. He probably thinks I'm insane. He turns back to me carefully and maybe a bit surprised. I don't recall anyone else questioning their readings.

"As I said, the answer to all your questions is true love." I can tell he is done with me. That's all I'm getting. True love? True love? I'm furious because I'm disappointed. I wanted a straight up actionable answer. A To Do List I could copy in my journal and go do. What the actual fuck am I supposed to do with that? True love is going to save the world? Great. Just great. What does this even mean? I want to stamp my feet and scream like a toddler.

Also, who is supposed to find true love? Me? God, I hope not. The boys in my grade are ridiculous and my parents aren't about to let me date anyone older. This is impossible. Why would Mrs. Carpenter wish true love on me at age 15? Is that even what that means? Mr. Carpenter? He's only been a widow for like a year. That's way too soon. Connelly would freak out if she knew Mr. Carpenter had like a girlfriend or whatever grown-ups call them. Connelly? She has Zach. I don't know that I'd call it true love per se, but they seem happy enough. He's an okay guy, I guess. They hang out a lot. I came here looking for answers about the President. How I could get her to believe in the science of climate change. Is she, President Robinson, the one who needs to find true love? What, I'm supposed to do? Get the President to just fall in love while she's running and ruining the free world? Who else would it be? Who else needs true love in order for me to save the world from complete and utter despair? The urge to throw a full on tantrum isn't going away. I clench my fists and imagine beating them into the soft blankets on my bed.

I slump in my chair. This is not what I was hoping for. Why can't the answer be something like: protest, stage a school strike, create a movement, become the voice of the science informed people, start a climate campaign, stage a coup, anything other than "true love."

The house lights come flooding on and everyone files out of the ballroom and spills out into the hallway, blinking in the bright artificial light. Head hanging, I make my way to the Grande Lobby doors to meet Khalil. He stands there with a sandwich and more ice cream for me. I'll give it to him, he knows me well. I can't help but smile when he hands me a soft serve that's as tall as my head. As he hands it to me, he quietly and quickly whispers, "She's right. Forgive yourself." The tender moment passes, and he's back to being Khalil. "Dude, you got a message! I started yelling at my phone and dancing around. People probably thought I was crazy. That was dope as hell, though."

"Yeah, it was cool, I guess. I mean, it means so much to me that Mrs. Carpenter came through just for me. FOR ME." My voice quivers. I don't say much more about that. There's no need to. What Mrs. Carpenter and Khalil gave me today are more than I could ever ask for. I should be head over heels joyful with Mrs. Carpenter's message. I take a minute to let that sink in. I'm so focused on my latest Big One, that I'm not giving myself enough space to really consider how amazing the past few minutes have actually been. The woman I killed, came back for me to tell me to forgive myself. Forgiveness. That's going to take some time. I've been working on it for a year, and I'm better but not forgiven. I close my eyes for a second and have a moment of gratitude. When I open my eyes, Khalil is looking at me sweetly. I swear I see tears in his eyes.

"I appreciate what just happened in there. I do. It was huge. Monumental. I need to process it some more. I honestly was just hoping for something simpler. Something more actionable. Something straight from the universe about the universe. But I don't know what I'm supposed to do with a message about true love."

"Yes, you do baby girl. You know what to do. I'm right here… with more ice cream," he smirks.

"Jesus, Khalil. It's never going to happen. This is serious. I have to save the whole fucking world. You know I do. You know how my dreams work. You now how messed up I've been for the past year. How can you still be trying to get with me right now? Are you even serious?" My voice is loud and my face flushes the color of strawberry sorbet. I'm annoyed at Khalil, but it's more than that. I'm frustrated and disappointed. I don't feel any closer to a plan than I was before Tyler Anderson, The East Coast Medium. I feel guilty for being mad. Fucking Grief Dragon. I should be so happy and peaceful right now from what Mrs. Carpenter gave me. Absolution. I feel like a brat, but I do think I still have a good reason to be freaked out. Mrs. Carpenter's absolution doesn't fix my other problem. SAVE THE WORLD NOW, SIMONE.

I also miss Connelly. It feels weird and hollow and shady that she's not here with me. I hate that she doesn't want to be part of this. She would know what to do or at least help me think it through. I also have no idea what to tell her about her mom. Her mom came to me. I didn't summon her or anything like that. BUT I HEARD from her mom. The person she avoids talking about or emoting about 97% of the time. Should I tell her? How will she react? Will she be happy? Will it help us get back to how we are truly meant to be? It seems like we've had this invisible thin line separating us just a bit since her mom died. And these days that line seems to be getting thicker.

Khalil is quiet after my outburst. He looks at me with pity in his eyes. "Listen, Simone, I'm your friend. I would do anything for you. Hell, I just roamed D.C. for three fucking hours trying to get a good enough signal so that dumbass buffering would stop, so that I could watch a weird-ass dude give messages from dead people because I didn't want you to have to do it alone." He catches his breath. "Even if I wasn't in there with you, I could still experience it with you, if that makes sense. That's why I livestreamed or tried to at least. Their signal was broke up in there. I didn't want you to be alone. I spent my whole Saturday on this whack ass plan of yours and, if I'm being honest, I loved it. Call me crazy," he blinks when he says this, an acknowledgment that he does think I am crazy, at least a little, but he keeps going. "I'll never stop pursuing you because I think you're amazing. But even if you never even so much as give me a peck on the cheek, I will still be your friend. I'll still stand by you. Like that old school song. I'll stand by you. I'll staaaand by you." He sings the last line to me. "You can't get rid of me by just showing out a little bit." He's looking me dead in the eye, but he's smiling at me now.

"I'm sorry," I whisper. "It's just not what I expected. I thought I would get a better answer. I'm just pissed and scared and completely floored by Mrs. Carpenter. It's a lot, you know. All of this. It's so much. Nobody gets how hard it is to be me. Nobody understands what it is like to be weird-ass me." He lets me have my pity party, but not all by myself. He reaches for my hand and I let him. It's the equivalent of a hug from Dr. A. Both are vital, more than I ever thought possible. We walk back to Union Station in silence. He's holds my hand and leads the way. The girl power in me says *I can do it myself*. The part of me that wants to be taken care of because life is hard as hell is grateful for the kindness. The beeps and horns of traffic and other delicious and obnoxious sounds of the city fill the space between us.

With my free hand, I hold my cone and lick my ice cream. The cool sweetness soothes me again. As the bus pulls away, Khalil turns to me.

"What if true love is the answer? And I don't mean you got to fall in love with me. You made it clear you don't want to. But maybe you could find true love with some other dude. He will suck way more than me, as you know, but you do you." He pauses and tussles my hair. I don't think anyone has every tussled my hair. I don't even know if that's a thing people do in real life. It's weird but not bad. And I don't know, like maybe the President needs true love too since she's the one that you're trying to convince of the science stuff anyways." He stops talking for a second and looks like he's figuring something out. He's so much smarter in so many ways that he lets on. I wish he knew that about himself. I should tell him something along those lines, but his lightbulb goes off suddenty and he keeps talking. "You know how sometimes the only person that can convince you of something is someone you got true love with? Like your dentist tells you to floss every day and you tell him you will but you don't. But then you get a girl, and you really, really like her. And you start brushing and flossing every day like you're a maniac about it. She convinces you to be better. You just like wanna be the best you can."

"First of all, that's disgusting. You really should floss every day. Second of all, you think I can just find true love? Easy peasy? And get the President OF THE UNITED STATES OF AMERICA to fall in love? Because that's such a common thing to do?"

"Nah, I don't think it's easy, but it could work. And, sorry baby girl but you didn't get a lot to work with. I'm just brainstorming here. But you're cool as hell. You can find a boyfriend. That's not gonna be that hard. Worst comes to worst, you can date me. I already love you." He tries to high five me, but I sit on my hands. Now both free of his hand and my ice cream. There is an awkward pause. We look at each other and then laugh. The laugh is a kind of knowing one like the cookoo lady's grin at the conference. The one who said I have everything I need. "Really though, I know you don't want to date me. I get it, but you could try dating other people. Connelly is great at stuff like hair and nails and being nice and all that. She could help you, you know, be like more dateable."

"What the actual hell is that supposed to mean?" I laugh though because it is true. Dating the boys at my school isn't a top priority. I'd rather be with Connelly or watching TV or even going to therapy over watching some dude play video games for hours. I don't get it. AT ALL. And for that reason I don't put a ton of time into stuff like nails and being cute and being nice or smiling for no reason. "Connelly doesn't want to help me with this plan. She says she can't right now. It's too much. I get it though."

"Okay, but like, she doesn't have to know its about the dream. Just tell her that she's been spending more time with Zach and you're kinda feeling left out or whatever and that you want, ummm..." He stops talking and is thinking again, "I know, you want like a makeover or whatever, like on those TV shows. *Queer Eye* and all those. She'll help you with that, plus then you can talk about the boys and dates and all that stuff with her... and not me. Please." His voice is softer than before. He clears his throat. "She loves that kind of shit. And she knows way more than you do. No offense."

No offense taken, really. That is actually a good idea. If I'm going to find true love, I'm going to need some coaching from Connelly and someone to talk to about it. I have no idea what to even do on a date. Or how to get those eyelash things on. Are those a requirement? It's going to take some work, but I can commit to trying to find true love. Without a little more instruction it seems like it could be what Mrs. Carpenter meant. I don't know. She would want me to be happy. I do know that. Maybe she thinks if I forgive myself and I find true love that I'll be happier. That seems logical. Maybe she can see a lot more from where she is now, the big picture. Like a birds eye view, if the bird lived in heaven. I'll put myself out there and give it a shot. I'll do my part to "find true love" since that is apparently the answer to everything. Connelly has her work cut out for her. That's for sure. She likes projects though. I can hear her forthcoming her squeals of delight already.

"Okay, okay. I think that's a possibility. I'm not thrilled about it, but what choice do I have? I have a lot riding on my interpretation of the message I was given. I have to take some risks, I guess. But what about the President? I think you might be on to something with the dentist thing. I mean I don't think she needs to go to the dentist, but what if she fell in love with someone who could convince her that everything the climate crisis science is telling us is true? What if that person could love her enough and she loves that person enough and her heart could get her brain to think differently? Is that possible? Is that like a real thing? Maybe she could love that person enough to want to save the planet so they can go on dates and vacation and stuff. Get married. Have a babies and whatever. "I'm in for Project..." my voice trails off as I think of a name. "Project Queen Canary." Khalil looks quizzically at me and asks, "What's that mean?"

I laugh because it *is* an unusual name. I guess I'm going to divulge my secret after all. "Other than Simon Alice Marker, my mom calls me Queen Canary. People used to say, *canary in a coal mine* because coal miners had canaries down in the mines to warn them of bad things coming. Canaries are super sensitive to bad conditions and feel them before people do. The canaries warned the miners when they were in danger. My mom says my dreams have been warnings letting us know when something bad is going to happen. I'm the queen of the canaries in the coal mine, I guess." "I have never heard of such a thing in my life," Khali sounds amused and slightly confused.

I just shrug and grin. I'm feeling less anxious. I look out the window. The sun is starting to set and the sky is beautiful. The train moves quickly and the sky flies by. I see every color that ever existed in that sky. It's like the whole history of the world is claiming its space in time and memory by sharing its gorgeous light once more before the day is done. It makes me do a triple breath. To think that the sky could only be black and polluted and never share its warm and cool colors again is heartbreaking. I'm not sure how all of this will work out, but I'm going to give it my best shot. I'm not going to be silent. I have a sky to save.

CHAPTER FIVE

Sunday, September 1

I spend the rest of the long weekend doing a shit ton of research like I told Dr. A I would do. I have Sunday and Monday to focus on it since we don't have school on Monday. I pull up website after website and am shocked at what I learn. I know that the climate crisis is bad, but I don't know the details. I subscribe to as many newsletters about the climate crisis as I can. I set up Google alerts. I want to know as much as possible. I follow people on the socials who are into climate change and are doing things about it. I want to be inspired and know what people are doing to help. I quickly join a network of influencers who are educated and action-oriented. I create new social accounts under the name @queencanary. I'm not sure why I do this when I have so many other parts of my plan to execute, but it's like I can't keep this information to myself. I want my friends and my city and my country and the world to see what's happening. Maybe the more people that know the truth, the more likely the President will have to listen to the science of it all. And in the meantime, maybe we can help make the world better without her. Maybe if enough people do their part, then we might still have a chance. It can't make it worse. Mr. Carpenter says we need the President, and I agree with him from what I'm learning. But maybe we need everyone else too. I begin posting the facts I find and tag @ThePresidentRobinson on everything I post. I also tag Mr. Carpenter's socials, @drewthedcscienceguy. No one knows it's me, so I don't think it is too weird. I add @khalil#1wrestler too. He's in it as much as I am at this point. I create tons of posts.

➤ *If cows were a country, they would be the third largest emitter of greenhouse gasses. #eatplants*

➤ *1/3 of food does not make it to your fork. #nomorefoodwaste*

➤ *Educate all girls. They run the world. More education, less climate crisis. #savetheplanet*

➤ *9,600 mail order catalogs are delivered every three seconds. 97% are thrown away the day the arrive. #nomorewaste #stopthesubscriptions*

➤ *The average American home uses 98 gallons of water each day. #switchtolowflow*

➤ *2/3 of the word's population lives in an area where water is severely scarce at least one month a year #waterscarcityawareness*

I'm embarrassed about how long I am online on Sunday. Once I start though, I can't stop though. Connelly asks me to come over but I tell her I can't. I blame it on my parents. She has plans with Zach on Labor Day, so I don't see her the rest of the weekend. I'm glad she has plans though. It gives me another day to do my research and think about my next moves. I text Khalil to let him know I've made a lot of progress on Project Queen Canary. He sends me the Thumbs Up and Heart emoji, plus a new song as he always does. Monday's song is something about girl power, which I like but don't tell him that. He follows my new socials. On Twitter, he retweets my posts. He also tags his dad who is some sort of high-powered D.C. attorney guy. Khalil says he's really into "the agenda" and that he'll like the information I'm sharing. I'm glad because we might need his help. He also thinks it will get his dad to think that he's focusing more on his school work. It serves us both well. We're a good team.

CHAPTER SIX

Tuesday, September 3

A t school on Tuesday, I'm excited to see Connelly. I miss her like crazy. I can't tell her everything about my plan, especially the part about her mom. At least not right now. The Guilt Dragon loves having that secret to torture me with. I might not be able to share all of that with her, but I can ask her to help me learn to date. You don't realize how much you need someone until you have to keep things from them. She's waiting for me at my locker per usual. A granola covered banana nut muffin in hand. My heart!

"Hi. I MIIIISSSS you!" I give her a big squeeze. She squeezes back. I ask her about her weekend. "How was your date with Zach yesterday? What did you do? Did you go somewhere?" She looks at me curiously and responds with her head cocked to one side and with a raised eyebrow.

"That's weird. You never ask me about my dates."

"I do so!" I exclaim weakly. I do not. Boys. Sigh. Whatever. But now I need to know how to do this lovey-dovey dating thing and fast. I am interested now. She rolls her eyes and says they had a great date with a picnic and making out and what not. Gross. This is going to be harder than I thought. As she talks, I study her face, clothes, hair, nails, and shoes. She dresses like a mom, very put together and … tailored. She's wearing a jean skirt that hits above the knee. Not too long, not too short. She pairs it with a white t-shirt. Not too tight, not too lose. She's got on white Chucks and they are actually *still* white and clean. A navy cross-body wraps around her upper body and holds her collection of lip-gloss and nail polish. Her hair, always curled in perfect loose curls, rests on her shoulders. She wears (everyday) matching blush, lip-gloss, and eyeshadow with a little mascara. Her nails are painted light pink with sparkles.

"Why are you looking at me like that?" I am staring at her. It's a fair question.

"You look nice that's all. Very tidy."

"Tidy? Great. Not exactly what I was going for, but could be worse, I guess."

"Connelly, what does Zach like about you're the most?"

"God, SAM, you're being so weird right now." She's right. I need a bit more tact. So many things to work on. She answers me in a voice I don't recognize.

"I don't know. My sparkling personality? The fact that I'm a little broken but still try really hard to be happy all the time. I don't know. Maybe because I really love being loved and need Zach in my life to fill a void the size of my mother." She sounds hollow and faraway.

Holy shit. Where did that come from? It's not that Connelly isn't ever sad. She is and has been off and on since her mom died, but only for like an afternoon or an hour at a time. She bounces right back and seems happier than ever. She never says stuff like this. She keeps things more to herself. She stays more on the surface. Like a buoy bobbing up and down in the water, no matter if it's rough or smooth.

"Umm, are you okay? Why did you say that? Did y'all have a fight? Is everything okay? Is Zach being good to you?" My defenses go up. Also, I sound just like my mother with this firing squad of questions. Geez. Talk about being normal.

She swallows and blinks slowly. "No, no, he's great. He is more than great. It's just, I know he and I spend a lot of time together. I need him. He makes me feel happier. I love when he kisses me and holds me. I feel safe and wanted with him. I know that sounds like a lot. I know you hate talking about stuff like that. That's why I don't bring it up much. Sorry." She shrugs a half shrug. It's like her light is dimmed today. She stops mid-sentence for less a second and then keeps talking. "I mean, I know I'm a little messed up since my mom died. I wish I didn't feel so dependent on Zach but I am. I'm sorry if I've been shutting you out a little."

She thinks she's been shutting me out, but I'm the one with a secret plan…that involves her widowed dad and her mother from the after-life. I hate myself right now. BE NORMAL. She keeps talking. "Is that why you're asking weird questions about Zach? Because I'm spending too much time with him?" In response to her question, I do something terrible. I lie to my best friend, and say yes and then I tell her that I really want a boyfriend badly so we can be equal again. I feel sick. I'm letting my best friend take the fall for something I need from her but can't even tell her. This does not feel good at all.

"Ok," she says brightening. "I can help! I know waaaaay more about boys that you do, and you could use a love coach. I'll text you some ideas later. This is going to be fun, like the time we got you ready for the 5th grade spelling bee. Remember how much we practiced your word list and your speaking voice and posture. And your mom made that sticker chart and kept track of your progress?" She giggles her precious little giggle at the memory and I force a smile.

"That would be great. I think it's time I act like a proper high-schooler." We talk for way too long and now we both have to run like freshman babies to first block. I don't feel good about the conversation for several reasons.

1. I don't like that I lie to Connelly AT ALL. I feel monstrous.
2. It was so unlike her to have such an emotional outburst like that. I'm worried about her. But also kind of glad she's getting her feelings out for once. Dr. A would approve.
3. I guess I didn't realize how serious things are with her and Zach. Probably because I *don't* ever really ask about him, but also because maybe she *has* been pushing me out. Maybe I just haven't realized it. I need to think more about this. Things are so complicated these days.

One thing I know for sure is that I need to keep an eye on her. She's been keeping an eye on me when I should have been there for her. I've been so fragile over the past year, but I'm strong now. I'm healthier too in so many ways. I can be there for her again. I wonder if she resents me for overdosing at a time when she was the one who should have been the sole focus of all of our time and energy. I need to add this to the list of stuff to talk about with Dr. A.

The day goes by quickly and I'm eager to get home and continue my research. I have so many questions after my research marathon from the weekend. I finish my homework in 90 minutes, which is pretty good. I keep my phone in my backpack so that I can focus on my English assignment without getting distracted. I'm quite proud of myself for this restraint and reward myself with three scoops of black cherry with hot fudge before I hunker down and work on Project Queen Canary.

I unlock my phone and go to Insta first. My Queen Canary account acquired over 300 followers since I started it yesterday. I used a lot of hashtags that combined climate change with local places and people and that seems to be working out okay. I repost a picture from the IG Search page that's trending. It's a picture of Simba with his dad. They are sitting together overlooking a desolate, polluted, smoldering city instead of a luscious green jungle. His dad tells Simba, "One day this will all be yours." I love Simba. Really I love Nala more, but Simba will do. I post with a warning that we are running out of time to save our beautiful home. I invite my followers to share the image and to get at least ten friends to follow the page. I promise that something special is coming soon, and they are going to want to be part of the solution and not the problem. I scroll through the hashtags I'm following on climate crisis and like a bunch of stuff. I make some comments too and get even more followers as people see what I'm liking and writing.

Before I move to Twitter, I have 200 more followers. I notice that a lot of my followers look my age. I grin. This is giving me hope. Also, BONUS, maybe one of these people can fall in love with me. That would be helpful. Of course, that won't work well since they don't know who Queen Canary is. Daaang it. I make a note to spend more time on the falling in love piece of my plan. I can't get overly focused in one area. There is so much to do. Breathe. Be normal. I pat my rabbit's foot.

I don't know why I'm shocked, but I find all sorts of hashtags and accounts that deny climate change and call it a hoax. A hoax! Must be these are the ones that President Robinsons follows. I take a deep breath on that one. I use my breathing exercises from Dr. Ambrossini to calm me down. In for four long, out for five longer. I get on Twitter and have another shock. Oh, shit. One of my tweets from yesterday is going viral. It's a picture of a skinny, ragged polar bear far from his home and he's crossing a busy highway in search of food. His eyes are hollow and he looks like death. I found the picture, cited the source, and wrote.

It's not his fault. It's yours. Today he's the one ravaging or food, tomorrow it's you. Wake up, world. Mother Earth is calling you, and she's pissed. Follow me for more information on the climate crisis and what you can do about it.

I don't think it's the words necessarily that get people going, but the image of that once gorgeous, royal is bear is enough to make anyone feel guilty enough to "like it."

The tweet has 50,000 likes and I now have over 10,000 followers on my twitter handle @queencanary. I jump up off the couch and do the lamest but most heartfelt happy dance of all time. I spend more time on Twitter following other accounts and hashtags. I retweet a bunch of facts and figures and sad pictures of what the earth will look like and what it already looks like right now. That part is terrifying to me. My belly churns at the facts. I realize I've been sitting for hours and decide to go for a run before I get dinner started. It's my night to cook. I'm making spaghetti…vegetarian spaghetti. My dad is going to ask where the meatballs are, but surprise—we're beef free from here on out. Got to cut down on our methane emissions. Woot Woot. Everybody do your part.

On my run, I pass by Khalil's house. It's on my normal route. I run up to the door and ring the bell. Mr. Williams answers it with gusto. I'm breathing heavy and sweating profusely. In Virginia, September is still as hot as the rest of the summer.

"Hey, Simone. How are you doing on this here fair evening?" He's still dressed from work in a midnight blue power suit. It hugs his muscular body. His shoes are shiny, sleek, and sturdy. I'm 5'10, which is super awkward when you're in tenth grade because it means I'm taller than most of the boys who haven't really, well, bloomed or whatever. Mr. Williams is not much taller than me, and he's built like a rhinoceros. No horn, but strong and thick. His muscles flicker under his expensive jacket.

"Good, Mr. Williams. Thanks. You?"

"Quite well, Simone. Quite well. Busy day at the office, but I'm glad to be home now."

"Cool. Is Khalil home?"

"Oh, you're not here to see me," he jokes in a fun way not a creepy way. He's really awesome. Serious and kind. "He's not home yet. Still at the gym. Not here studying." He rolls his eyes in a grand gesture of annoyance, but keeps the friendly smile on his face.

"Oh, yeah. He's really into that, huh. I thought he might be back by now though. He should really buckle down, huh?" I say that for Mr. William's benefit. I think Khalil has it figured out more than the rest of us do. Does it really matter if you get a B or a C instead of an A on everything? Does it? I'm starting to think it doesn't, and that Khalil is way happier by having balance in his life. I don't bring this up to Mr. Williams. I get the feeling Khalil's dad has gotten A's on everything he's ever done.

Mr. Williams laughs. "Yes, he should. I'm on him all the time. Encouraging him to focus on his school work. It's not his cup of tea, as you know." He pauses. "He does seem to be taking a keen interest in his science project though. It's on climate change. He's suddenly very into it. He tagged me in a bunch of tweets yesterday about the climate crisis, which was quite odd. He normally ignores me on all of the social media outlets. He acts like he's never heard of his old dad. I tell him all the time that most kids would be pretty stinking proud to have a dad like me. Not too many guys out here like me trying to change the world one high profile case at a time." I nod my head in agreement. I'm happy to play along. He deserves it. Especially since he puts up with Khalil.

"You're the best, Mr. Williams. He'll come around. He told me you might be happy about the tweets."

"Oh, are you into the climate crisis too, Simone?"

Oh shit. I said too much. Of course it would be weird for two teenagers to be sitting around talking about climate change and tweeting about it. I don't want anyone to know I'm Queen Canary. I'm trying to be a normal kid for once, not a geeked out science fanatic.

"Oh, no, I mean. We were just talking about him studying more and focusing more on his schoolwork and stuff. He said he was working on a research paper for his science class and had found a bunch of environmental stuff that he thought you'd like. He wants to make you proud, Mr. Williams. That's all."

"He does, does he? Well, that's news to me."

I shrug and nod. Not sure what else to do. Then it's awkward, so I tell him I have to get going. Got to keep my heartrate up! He says he'll have Khalil reach out when he *finally* gets home from the gym. I run back home as fast as I can. My to-do list hanging over my head with no time to lose.

I have fun making our dinner. I crank up the speaker and let John Mayer and the Dead and Co. serenade me as I cook. I feel in charge. I'm happy. After our meatball free spaghetti dinner, my phone lights up with texts from Connelly.

after therapy on fri meet me at the salon

why

just do it
Khalil said you want a makeover
that's a good place to start w getting a boyfriend!
guys will notice a change
ill get you some of the lashes
lol

I don't text back right away. I have to get a makeover to get a guy? I didn't realize Khalil was suggesting that I actually need to up my game on the outside. Although, Connelly says it's her sparkling personality that Zach likes. I wouldn't use the word *sparkling* to describe mine per se. Maybe I do need to do some hair and nail things or whatever. Do it for the planet, SAM. Do it for the planet. I raise my fist to the universe and shake it dramatically. Here's to you Tyler Anderson, The East Coast

Medium. I think about the Sixth Sense Conference. I take a moment to consider what Mrs. Carpenter said to me about forgiving myself. I still haven't worked through that. Can I? Can I really forgive myself? It seems like it will be much easier to do if I can save everyone else. A penance to pay.

if i have to

tell your dad we'll be late

i don't want to eat cold bean burgers

yes!

right will do

this is going to be so much fun

you'll see

I send her the monkey covering its eyes emoji. Yeah, we'll see.

I spend the rest of the week learning more and more about the climate crisis. As it turns out, we are in big trouble. We treat the planet like we live on 1.65 of a planet instead of just one, which means we are over consuming Mother Earth and all her resources faster than we are replenishing them. Alaska had its hottest summer ever and Europe is baking. They don't even have air conditioning there! I can't imagine spending one night in Virginia's summer heat without AC to cool me down. I'm learning though that emissions from refrigerants, the stuff that makes AC cool, are terrible for the environment. Ain't that something? The environmental stuff is pretty crazy and devastating, but I also learn about the pure chaos that will occur if we continue to deplete the planet. Everyone will become desperate for resources like food and water and they will do whatever it takes to get what they need—kill, kidnap, and even start wars. Daaaammnnn.

I learn about the circular economy. I had no idea such a thing existed. I thought recycling was enough. Apparently, it's not. We need to only take or buy what we need, then return it or recycle or reuse it or repair it. So that each item is a forever item. Every single thing is totally consumed. It never makes it to a landfill or to the trash. Dadgumit. I have some work to do on that one. I think about all the stuff that I waste. Tons of stuff every day. I feel bad. I didn't know. More people need to know. I'm inspired to keep sharing what I'm finding out. Each one teach one. I have a mission. I have to complete it before it's too late.

The research also gives me hope. I learn that when we started working on the hole in the ozone, there were a bunch of people who thought the idea was complete garbage. Now the hole is actually getting smaller! Together we can make a difference. I think about my polar bear picture and tell him I'm sorry for what we did to him, but that I'm going to make it better. I have to.

By the time Friday rolls around, I'm eager to see Dr. A. It's really stressful and exhausting to learn so much depressing information. My head and my neck hurt, maybe from stress, maybe from spending too much time on my phone. I also feel kinda alone right now. Khalil never texted me back this week after I went to his house. He only sent me a couple of songs too; he didn't send one every day like he normally does. Not sharing any of this with Connelly or my parents is isolating. Isolation is not great for people with brains like mine. I think I want to be alone with my thoughts, but then it is too much. When I get too isolated, I get depressed. I can't let that happen. I also need to talk to her about Mrs. Carpenter's forgiveness message. I want to accept it so badly, but I'm not sure how to yet. I need her help processing it. I need to talk to Dr. A.

As always, she is happy to see me and I dive right into how I'm doing and what I'm feeling. I start with the Sixth Sense Conference and Mrs. Carpenter's message. It's weighing on me as much as the climate stuff. When I tell her about the forgiveness message, even Dr. A bursts into tears.

"Simone, I've been telling you that same thing! Just like your parents have and Connelly has. Now you've heard it from her yourself. It's time that you accept that forgiveness and cloak yourself in it. There are no more excuses. How are you feeling about the gift she gave you?" Her voice is full of love and tenderness. She's basically pleading with me to fully accept what Mrs. Carpenter gave me.

"I feel grateful. I do. I really do. It means so much to me. It was so real and genuine. I'm having a hard time accepting it of course. She's still dead and it's still my fault. I guess I can't really separate those things."

"Perhaps not yet, Simone, but you have to do that work. You have to keep pulling apart what happened. I know you feel responsible, but Connelly is right. These things do happen. You speaking up may or may not have prevented Mrs. Carpenter's cancer and death. We will never know, and that's okay. Especially now. Simone, you are absolved. It's up to you now to embrace loving yourself enough to forgive yourself. Everyone else already has. You have to choose it for yourself."

My throat closes in on itself. I nod because it is easier than trying to say something. I know she's right. I know it in my head, but getting my heart to love myself enough to stop fighting the Guilt Dragon feels impossible. We sit in silence for a few minutes. Dr. A is really good about knowing when to be quiet. When I can speak again I tell her, "I think that once I do what I need to do about my latest Big One, then I know for sure that I can forgive myself. I don't know if I can do it before then, but I will try. I know it is important to getting better and staying better."

She nods and writes something in her notes. She's calm and careful, emitting grace and forgiveness. She's a good role model. After another quiet moment, I thank her for what she said and then I tell her about everything else.

After I bring her up to speed on all my planning, she says,

"I can see you're quite passionate about your plans, Simone. I am worried though that you are going at this alone. What you're taking on is a great responsibility. Who do you know that can help you with your plans?" I bite my bottom lip, and bite it hard. I scroll through my plans:

1. Get the President to find true love
2. Get myself to find true love
3. Learn as much as I can about the science of climate change
4. Get other people to learn as much as they can about climate change
5. Act normal! Don't be a freak.

I tell her that I feel pretty good about the *finding true love for myself* plan. Connelly is on it. We even have some sort of makeover date happening today after my session. I also have a few other ideas like using a dating app and, well, there's always Khalil. IF I HAD TO, maybe I could make that work? I shudder at the thought, mostly out of habit, but I also smile a little.

My research is going well. I tell Dr. A that I feel less alone on the socials and in the Twittersphere than I do in real life. She tells me that's nice and all, but as we are humans living a real life, we need real life humans doing life with us. She challenges me again to consider who can help me. A real live person that I can sit down with and share some of my anxiety and heavy feelings of responsibility. I promise her that I will get some more real humans onboard.

I'm stuck when it comes to getting to the President to make her find true love. I just don't know about this part of the plan yet. I ask her for some time, and I tell her that I'll report back next week. We talk some more about the anxiety I'm feeling over the weight of Project Queen Canary. I ask her if I'm crazy. I wonder why I have to be so awkward and weird. Why I have to dream these things that come true? I ask her why I can't just be normal? I don't cry though. Shocking, I know.

I'm not sad or depressed. I am too determined to be down right now. I just wonder what it would be like to not feel the weight of my dreams, especially this one. Dr. A is the best. She assures me that I'm not a freak. She doesn't call my power a power, she says I see things that others don't because I am "intuitive." She says there is nothing wrong with being in touch with my subconscious and the invisible energies that surround us. She reminds me that it takes a special brain to be able to process and manifest the secrets of the universe. She has a way of making me feel special and not like a psycho.

We practice thinking about my emotions and reframing them when they start to run away with me. She says I have more power over my mind than I know. Once I see that a feeling or an emotion or a thought is taking over too much, I can reign it in by seeing it, naming it, and then choosing something different. Then we practice changing what I do based on what I'm *thinking* more so than what I'm *feeling.* This gives me more control. I feel better when I'm taking action on my plan and not just freaking out about it. I feel confident and peaceful even while I feel responsible and heavy. I'm learning that it's hard to ever just feel one thing at a time. She also reminds me that I am chosen. I have been hand selected by the universe to see this plan through. She encourages me to keep talking to her and she insists I confide in my parents. She reminds me that they are on my side. They have seen the power of my "intuition" and don't question my abilities. I know she's right. I need them.

I leave therapy and head to the salon. I have no idea what Connelly has in store for me. I have to save the world, but I'm just as nervous about these salon shenanigans she's got planned. I meant to watch one of those makeover shows that Khalil mentioned to get a better idea of what this is going to be all about, but I got caught up in my research. I'm in for a surprise, for better or for worse.

Most days, I put my long straight plain brown hair into a ponytail or a braid down my back and just go with it. Technically I *have* make-up (Connelly gives it to me), but I don't wear it much. It feels gross on my skin. I can actually feel it just sitting there on the surface of my face like an extra layer of filth that I just don't need in my life. I paint my nails about once a year, then it 1.5 days later they are already chipping, and it's time to do the again. That's insane. One you paint them, they should stay that way forever. If you have to sit still that long, it should be a guarantee. I just don't have patience for that nonsense.

I hesitate when I open the salon's door. It smells like eucalyptus and sulfur. It's not a great combo. Connelly actually squeals when I walk in. She grabs me by the arm and marches me to a "hair artist" named Tiffany. Tiffany takes one look at me and claps her hands together like a cheerleader after a touchdown. I'm honestly a little scared. The next two hours are a boring blur. I don't know what is happening, and I'm not allowed to move or open my eyes. There's a lot of poking and prodding on my face and on my head. I hear what sounds like thin pencil shavings hitting the tile floor. Now I'm straight up terrified. I haven't had a haircut since freshman year. That's kind of gross, I know. It just isn't that important to me. And again, there's a lot of sitting still for a haircut. I'm starving. Even the black bean burgers sound delicious right about now. I'm antsy. I don't ever sit still this long. After what seems like three days of torture, Tiffany spins me around to see her masterpiece. She actually says that.

Holy shit. My hair falls in what I think are called layers. They cascade around my shoulders. They look soft and flowy. My hair is now the color of a shiny Hershey's bar not just plain, flat brown. I must be hungrier than I thought if now my hair looks like food. No more plainness. It's so shiny I can see my reflection in it. Is that even right? Connelly points out that that the summer sun had given my hair an old, dull penny-like hue. It's much better now she assures me. Now it is one gorgeous sheen of brown. She's very pleased with herself. I guess she's right. I wish someone would have told me my hair turned to ugly penny. I didn't know.

My eyebrows look very…organized. They normally have more, well let's just say, character. They are spunky and have a mind of their own, if you will. Now they are lined up in perfect arches. Are they permanent? Am I expected to be able to re-create these little brown rainbows all on my own? I have more make-up on now than I have ever worn in my entire life. My face is four different colors, like a topography map. I see golden brown, dark peach, shimmery rose, and…is that like silver glitter? Yes, I have silver glitter ON MY FACE. Glitter. On *my* FACE. My lips are the color of the inside of a cherry. I'm not mad at that though. Of all the new things about my face and head, the shiny, opaque red on my lips is my favorite. I think I can sustain putting on lip-gloss as long as that's all there is to it. The rest of the makeover is a huge mystery wrapped in an enigma. How did they do that? How will I do that? Do I have to do that? I take a deep breath. I look a little harder and a little longer.

I peer at myself longer than necessary. No one ever says I'm pretty, expect my mom and my Granny. No one ever says I'm ugly either though, and given the world domination of The Internet Trolls, I'm glad for that. I'll chalk that up to a win. Assuming Connelly is right about this makeover thing, then I think a boy might think I'm pretty right now. I'm not sure I think that though. I can't tell. I like what I see in the mirror. It's very nice. I'm just not sure I like it for me. Who is this version of Simone Alice Marker? I'm still the same person, right? I keep looking to see if I recognize myself. On the other hand, Connelly and Tiffany are pleased as punch. They are jumping up and down in little circles, pumping their arms in victory.

"Stay right there! Just like that!" Connelly pulls out her phone and begins Snapchatting the unveiling of the new me. I doubt my expression is very warm, inviting, or cheerful. Then again models aren't either, so maybe that's good. I stare blankly at Connelly's phone while she does her thing. She shrieks. "So many people are seeing this! I'm sending it to everyone. I'm adding it to my story right now. Ok, I'm starting a group chat with some guys I have in mind for you." She sounds downright joyful. I'm exhausted. I also feel a little cheap. Is this what it comes down to in order to find true love? Layers and lipstick and Snapchat filters, oh my?

Mr. Carpenter picks us up from the salon. I'm grateful for the ride even though it's a short walk. I need a nap. On the way home, Connelly keeps adding to her story and sending Snaps. Mr. Carpenter notices her gleeful mood and tries to join in, but he is distant and much quieter than normal. He doesn't even notice that I look like a completely different person. Once Connelly is satisfied with her *SAM Got a Makeover* advertisements, she finally notices that her dad isn't himself.

"Daddy, what's wrong?" There's a slight panic in her voice. I guess you would be more guarded after what she and her dad have been through.

"Nothing, honey. I'm fine really. I'm just tired. It's been a long week." He looks in the rearview mirror to catch her eye. He nods assumingly at her. He does look tired. He looks the way I feel.

"DAD. I know you better than that. I'm sorry I was so absorbed in my phone. I should have noticed. What's the matter? Tell me. I put my phone away." She tucks her phone under her thigh. It sticks out a little so she can see the screen light up.

"Ah, honey, you got me. You do know me well." He manages a chuckle. "Well, actually, sweet pea, I do have some news for you. Well, I, uh, I guess I got a new job today." He lifts his voice at the end of his announcement to indicate enthusiasm. My first thought is all about me. Immediately, I am scared to death that my Connelly is going to move from Longview and away from me. Selfish, much?

"Dadddddy," she extends the word and her voice is high. "Congratulations! That's awesome, right? New jobs are a good thing. Why are you sad though? What's the job? Tell me!" She encourages him to say more.

"Well, honey, you know how President Robinson sometimes fires people abruptly when she doesn't like what they have to say or how they say it? Well, she's gone through three Administrators of the EPA in the past two years. She let another one go earlier in the week. She says she has her reasons. I'm sure she does. The ranks are thin right now when it comes to possible candidates for the job. With so few viable options, she apparently asked me to be appointed to the job. You're looking at the new Administrator of the Environmental Protection Agency."

Connelly and I look at each other. We don't know if this is good or bad news. We shrug. I nod at her to say something. It sounds important. It's music to my ears. I think this might be the kind of thing I need working in my favor for my plan to be successful. The EPA is a really important part of saving the planet. Now, Mr. Connelly is going to be in charge of it. He'll have the President's ear. The universe does conspire with me. I tap my rabbit's foot three times as a thank you.

"Daddy, that sounds like a great opportunity." She looks at me to check in. I nod again encouraging her to go on. "You've been working really hard for the EPA for a long time, right? You are probably the best person for the job. Don't you think? I think this is good news." She crosses her fingers and gives them a slight waggle in my direction. He sighs quietly. "It's a great opportunity to do the right thing and to have an impact on the environment. I have always dreamed of having this job. I never thought it would be possible though. I thought taking time off and stepping back from my career back when your mom got sick would keep me from ever having the chance. It's bittersweet." My stomach tightens. Life is hard for everyone at some point in time or another. "But here we are, I have the opportunity of a lifetime with the most difficult project of a lifetime to go with it. Ain't life grand?" He laughs as he says this but it's not a *haha* laugh. It's more of an ironic scoff. It's very un-Carpenter-like.

We arrive at their house, and Mr. Carpenter goes to the kitchen to finish making dinner. He mumbles something about FRYday and then disappears around the corner. I don't follow him this week. He seems like he needs some space. Connelly grabs me by the hand and we got upstairs to her room. We plop down on two big beanbags, dropping our book bags on the floor beside us.

"I haven't seen my dad this emotional in a long time. He's been doing so good. We "do good" for each other more than for ourselves. For him to be upset about such a great job, President Robinson must be a real...peach. Maybe she needs to get laid." As soon as she says this very un-Connelly-like statement, she blushes the color of my new lip-gloss. She looks away from me and unlocks her phone to check Snapchat. What is with the Carpenters today? I'm honestly a little freaked out by Connelly's weird outbursts lately. She seems to be cracking a little bit. I know a lot about cracking. My cracks have been craters. Hers seem to be hairlines for now. I need to keep an eye on her though. I take a deep breath. There are so many things that I need to focus on. My brain feels like a monkey lives in there and is swinging from branch to branch, calling out *hoo hoo haw haw hoo hoo haw haw* at the top of his lungs every time he swings. Each thought of what I need to do or what I'm worried about is another swing, another *hoo hoo haw haw*. I'm also embarrassed. I don't know much about getting laid. I have only kissed three boys. Those kisses are as far as I've gotten around the proverbial bases. I'm not exactly sure what Connelly even means. Why would she say that like that about the President?

On the other hand, her weird statement reminds me of what Khalil said about the dentist. Maybe the President really does need some love in her life. I'm not sure about the sex part, but it seems like adults generally have both in a package deal. Maybe I could clue Connelly into my plans to help the President find true love under the guise of getting the Prez to chill out and be nice to her dad? I would still be lying to her a little bit, but at least we could work on it together. I need all of my best friend back. I hate doing something this important without her by my side.

As I'm thinking about what that could look like, something dawns on me. What if Mr. Carpenter could be the guy? What if he's the President's true love? Maybe Mrs. Carpenter really wants Mr. Carpenter to be happy again. Maybe she just really wants to help Mr. Carpenter find his way back to love. He and Mrs. Carpenter were so happy together. I have a million memories of them cooking, taking walks, reading the newspaper, driving Connelly and me to D.C. to go to the zoo and to every exhibit at every museum. I'm certain Mr. Carpenter loving up on the President of the United States isn't exactly what Connelly has in mind when she says she should get laid, but that's a minor detail. It's a win-win. The President finds true love. Mr. Carpenter does too, and he's back to his *happy all the time* self again. I get what I need to save the planet from the stupid, stupid climate crisis. We all win! I need to figure out how to get Connelly to help me.

As I scheme, Connelly goes through her chats. Suddenly, she's on her feet exclaiming, "SAM, you're not going to believe this. Come here. Look at this." She's pointing furiously at her phone. I can't see anything through her flailing. "What? What is it? Jesus, Connelly. You scared me." I'm afraid she read my mind and is pissed as hell at my plan to get the President to fall in love with her recently widowed dad. Oh wait, wait. Wait a minute, I'm the one with psychic powers. *Ha ha*. A little industry joke. "Langdon Harris wants to know *who this is!*" She points at my picture on her phone. "THE LANGDON HARRIS. As in soccer stand out, sophomore class council, Langdon Harris. He saw my story and he wants to know who that is!" I am confused at first, but then realize she's talking about me. He doesn't recognize me.

"Connelly, he's known me since the 4ᵗʰ grade. How can he

not know who I am?" Then I remember that I look like an alien version of myself in her stories. "Oh my god, Connelly. That's insulting. I have literally known him since I had a SpongeBob SquarePants lunch box. This is ridiculous. I'm so embarrassed."

"Don't be. This is so awesome. I'm so proud of myself. I made you unrecognizable. I knew I could do it." She makes her hand into a little fist and draws it down into her side with a little "yes."

Geez. Could she be overdoing it slightly? She's making a strong statement over there. I don't think I was that bad off before. Do I really need to be unrecognizable?

"Could you tell him that it is me? Someone that he has known since he moved here? The person who carried his ass through our 6th grade science fair project when Mrs. Hernandez made us be partners even though he *cried* when he pulled my name out of the hat?" I am straight up whining right now. Again.

"Oh, stop it. Langdon knows who you are. He's just surprised by how pretty you look."

"Connelly, is that supposed to make me feel better or worse? I am fine with the way I looked before. Honestly, I really want my hair back. I feel naked."

"Stop being so sensitive! Of course, you always look very....SAM. Very SAM-like. You're very on brand. Now you've just had a little brand refresh."

I have no idea what that means. It doesn't feel like a compliment, but Connelly doesn't have a mean bone in her body. We just have different priorities. She likes to look like a grown up, like a put together adult, and I like to look like I woke up like this.

"Come with me and my dad to D.C. tomorrow for Khali's pre-season wrestling tournament thingie-do. I'll invite Langdon to come with us. He's known Khali as long as he's known you and your SpongeBob SquarePants lunchbox." She's smiling with her eyes and still pointing at her phone emphatically. Against my very best judgement, I agree to this seemingly very bad idea.

CHAPTER SEVEN

Saturday, September 7

Mr. Carpenter drives us to D.C. and we pick Langdon up on the way. I've never felt more awkward. Mostly because I try hard to recreate Tiffany's hair masterpiece and it doesn't go well. I attempt to style it while Connelly is in the shower. She isn't able to salvage much of my effort. I have no idea how to do shorter hair. Today the layers are jagged and not flowy. How did she do that? A braid down my back is not happening for a long time. The make-up isn't terrible. I skip all the colors and opt for a swirl of the dark peach and a light slick of the cherry gloss. I can tell by the look on Langdon's face that he's expecting Snapchat Simone and not Standard Simone. Thankfully, he sits up front with Mr. Carpenter and they talk about Virginia football. I have nothing to add to the conversation. Connelly and I sit in the back and talk about the Homecoming dance coming up in a few weeks.

We get to the wrestling tournament in time to see Khalil's first match. He's thrilled that we're there. When he catches my eye, he points to his head to indicate *hair* and gives me big thumbs up. The gym smells like popcorn and teenage boy sweat. Sweet and salty. Heavier on the salt. We sit with Khalil's parents. Khalil's dad may want him to buckle down at school, but he seems pretty stoked to see him pin his guy in the first period. There's a lot of "that's my boy" and loud heckling of the ref for a bad call in the first minute of the match. Langdon comes to sit between Connelly and me after Khalil's match is over. We get permission (for Connelly really) to walk to down the street to get lunch. Khalil doesn't have another match for another two hours. That's the thing about wrestling; they are an all-day affair with just minutes of your guy doing anything at all. It's a big commitment to be a fan.

We walk towards the National Mall to eat at The Pavilion. As we get closer, we see 7th street crowded with people protesting. As we get closer we see their signs and banners. They are opposing police brutality. Langdon makes a shitty comment to the effect of *if you don't do anything wrong, you don't have to worry about getting your ass kicked*. I catch Connelly's eye and I shake my head NO. I clap back, "Trayvon wasn't doing anything wrong. Tamir wasn't doing anything wrong. Michael wasn't doing anything wrong. They are dead, Langdon. It's more complicated than just doing the right thing. Obviously not all cops are bad. That's stupid to think. There are tons of them who are great, but what these people are protesting is a real issue. A serious, life or death issue." I think of Khalil and how his life is different than Langdon's. Langdon will never have to worry about wearing a hoodie or eating Skittles from his pocket. He'll never have to carefully and swiftly put his hands up to show they are empty. He'll never have to say firmly but still politely, *don't shoot*. I can feel the heat emitting from my body. My fury is radiating from my head, cheeks, and hands. Khalil may drive me insane, but he's taught me about a lot of things I never would have known.

"Woah, woah. Calm down, Simone. Jesus." Langdon uses his arms to indicate that I settle down, like he's pushing me back to where I came from. Not a great idea, Langdon. Not great. I think about telling my mom to calm down and send her a silent, *I'm sorry*. It is really a terrible thing to say to someone when they are in their feelings. He continues, "Seriously, calm down.

Don't get your pretty little panties in a wad. I didn't mean it like that. I just mean, do the right thing and everyone is chill."

"Everyone is not chill, Langdon. That's so stupid. Do you even ever read?" Oh my god, I can't with this guy. I don't think this quasi-date is going so well. I would never even kiss a boy like Langdon, much less fall in love with him. We sit down for lunch and Connelly does her best to carry the conversation. I appreciate her efforts, but I really just want to walk back to the auditorium by myself. The conversation is stiff and uncomfortable. I watch the protestors from our table. I am sending them all my good vibes, and I'm happy I can see them. On the walk back to the gym, Connelly walks ahead of us and Facetimes Zach, leaving me to walk alone with Langdon.

"Listen, Simone. I'm sorry. I didn't mean to upset you. Sometimes I just say stuff that I hear my parents say and I don't even know if I believe it myself. You're probably right." He stops and turns to me. Without thinking, I take a step back. "Give me another chance. Let me take you out after the game on Friday. We'll go to The Jukebox. It'll be fun. A bunch of the soccer guys will be there. They're cool."

"I'm busy. I do FRYdays with Connelly and Mr. Carpenter. We eat fries," I say flatly. "I can't." His reprieve to a decent human being is short lived. "Jesus, Simone. Grow up. You can't do that stuff forever. We're in high school now. You need to act like it." He doesn't deserve any more of my energy. In my mind, I completely dismissed him. Now I just need to get away from him forever.

We keep walking and but don't say anything else. I think about the protestors. They get our attention. They make their point. They cause a first date fight. I wonder if I can stage a protest. I want to. I have wanted to do something like that since I started my research. It seems like a good way to get other people thinking and talking. That's part of my plan. Part of what I have to do. People need to know *now* about the climate crisis.

They need to change *now*. We can't sit around waiting for some-one to save us. My socials are blowing up. I'm posting stuff every day and getting thousands of followers. I keep tagging the President and people connected to her. This morning on the way to the tournament, I tagged Mr. Carpenter again too. My plans are colliding. I decide I'm definitely going to protest. Thanks for the inspo, 7th Street protestors.

CHAPTER EIGHT

Wednesday, September 11

Every year on September 11, my parents keep me home from school and we go to D.C. for memorial services and events. The Carpenters go too. It means a lot to our family to honor the victims of September 11. I've lived in Longview my whole life. Our friends were at the Pentagon. Our neighbors helped with rescue and rebuild. A lot of people commute to D.C. from Longview, and several people from our town were murdered that day. My parents are hell-bent on keeping their memory alive. They talk openly to me about issues like terrorism. Maybe mom's serial morning news rants teach me more than I realize.

This year is no different. We head to D.C. and run the 911 Heroes race together. Well, we start together, I should say. I smoke my mom. My dad is faster than both of us. Connelly walks. Mr. Carpenter walks with her. He's not the kind of person to compete. He's just cool being who he is, where he is, doing what he does. Connelly doesn't like to sweat. The curled hair and all. Then we volunteer at a food panty near the Pentagon. After we finish there, we go to the Pentagon Memorial where the President is giving a speech. This is a golden opportunity. I need to strike. After the run, we eat a snack and chat. I corner Mr. Carpenter.

"How's the new job?" I immediately feel like a fraud. What fifteen year old asks someone's dad about their job? Even if he is a like a second father to me.

"Well, kiddo. That's nice of you to ask. I haven't done much yet though. But so far, so good. It's only been a few days, you know. I haven't had a chance to meet with the President face to face yet, but she did invite me and some others to an event after her speech this evening. I'm looking forward to having some one on one time with her. I've been putting a lot of thought into it, and I'm going to give it my best shot. Getting to know the President, respecting her, and sharing with her the facts are my best bet to save the world." Little do you know, Mr. C. Little do you know. I'm counting on you. The whole world is counting on you.

I tilt my head and nod it like I'm really engrossed in what he's saying. It's not hard to do since I have a vested interest that he doesn't know anything about. "I've been doing a lot of research, Mr. Carpenter, for science class," I add quickly to give myself a reason for geeking out about the environment. "We need you and the President to save the planet! I think you're the one for the job. She seems reasonable about a lot of other topics. She negotiated a health care plan that everyone agrees with, right? I think you can do it. Together, I mean. You two as like a power couple, uh, team. You can do it, together. Also, she's really pretty. Don't you think?" This last part is a stretch, but I have to plant seeds.

"A power couple, huh. Well, I hadn't thought about us like that, I can assure you. I have noticed that, yes, she is quite beautiful." He's smiling like I'm a cute little kid. Ugh. "There's no doubt about that. She's got Jackie O's classic style and Michelle's confidence, charm, and intelligence. And far more importantly, yes, her negotiations between both parties to settle health care reform during her presidency is one of the most amazing things I've ever seen in my life. You're right. She is reasonable. I am going to get to know her and figure out how to

meet her where she is. Maybe, I'll talk with the healthcare committee and find out how they did it. That's a great idea, Simone.
Thank you for that! Logic. Facts. And what worked before!" Add
a little love to that logic, if you don't mind.

I don't get to stick around to see how the event goes because I wasn't invited. Not everyone gets to hang out with the
President, I guess. Connelly comes home with us since her dad
will be late. We get a mid-week school-night sleepover, my favorite. It feels like I have a real sister when we do regular life
stuff together like get ready for school and pack lunches. Plus
she's going to help me do my hair. I need the help. She says she's
bringing a bag of tricks to spruce me up. I think that means
make-up, but I don't know for sure. Since things don't work
out with Langdon, I have to keep trying. In the car on the way
home from the 911 services, Connelly and I set me up on Yubo.
Connelly uses the pictures she took of me at the salon to fill in
the profile. We start swiping and soon, I'm chatting with a boy
named Stephen Zagros. He goes to All Saints with Khalil and
lives in Longview, but I don't know him. Connelly texts Khalil.

what do you know about stephen zagros

                                    sup cuz
                                      why

SAM yubo

                                       ah
                    still tryin to get my girl a date
                    tell her to come to the source
                              the good stuff
                                  i got her

STOP

                                he alright

kinda dorky

plays the horn or some shit

dorky is good

for simone

lol

lol

cant believe he does yubo

he never talks

maybe hes shy

i always thought he was just a big nerd

suits her

c you @ sun dinner

luv you cuz

heart emoji

"He's good, SAM. Nice guy. He plays in the band. You'll like him. Ask him out."

"Ask him out? Ask him out to where?" I want to whine, but I try not to. It's not very becoming.

"SIMONE. This is not that hard! Let's go to the football game tomorrow night after FRYday dinner. He can't come because of band or whatever, so we can meet up afterwards at The Jukebox. You can get the hot fudge brownie sundae. Even if the date is bad, you'll at least be happy dessert. Zach and I will go with you."

I sigh. I remember telling Langdon that I can't go to the Jukebox on Friday, but I shrug and agree. I reach for my rabbit's foot and pet it for a few seconds. I'm tired from the emotion of the day and the race. I have to keep trying to find true love. The world is depending on me after all. We set it up. No rest for the weary. I send Stephen a message through Yubo to set it up.

We send a few more messages back and forth. Honestly, he does seem nice. He tells me about his band friends, and we swap stories about what we do to remember 9/11. He's very polite. How bad can it be?

CHAPTER NINE

Thursday, September 12

Mom makes us breakfast and snarls at the TV while I eat and Connelly finishes getting ready upstairs. More news. More bad news. Then the next segment starts. They show a clip from the President's speech at the Pentagon yesterday and footage from the event afterwards. There are a lot of people there. When I realize what the clip is about, I lean in close to the TV and shush my mom. She doesn't like that one bit. I watch Mr. Carpenter. He doesn't take his eyes off the President the whole time she's speaking. She *is* captivating. On the topic of September 11, she's generous, kind, and empathetic. When she's done she makes her way through the people standing near the stage. Mr. Carpenter is near the makeshift ramp as she exits. She shakes hands and nods gravely to the crowd. When she gets to Mr. Carpenter, he leans in, bends down so that his mouth meets her ear and says something. I can see his mouth move. Just a few words. The President stops, looks over her shoulder quickly, nods, and then hurries on to the next person waiting in line.

What was thaaaat? I'm dying! I'm so curious I can barely stand it. I don't say anything though because Connelly enters the room. I need to get her involved in my plan, but how? We could be having the best conversation right now about her dad and our Madame President. She sits down beside me and snatches the last strawberry from my plate. My family is going plant based after all my research. No more bacon. I miss bacon. So much. The sacrifices we make.

The station is about to go to commercial. Before it does, the newscaster reminds us that *tomorrow is Friday the 13th and to BEWARE*. I close my eyes and take a deep breath. I will not let that the anchor take away from the good feeling I'm feeling. I am hopeful. I also feel a little manic, but that's normal for me. I need to compose myself. There's been a part of me that's thought that my whole plan is way too big and unruly to work. There's something about the intimacy of the interaction between Mr. Carpenter and the President though that stirs me. Hope. The thing with wings. I feel a little like flying, like maybe I'm not in this alone. That the powers behind my dream are the same powers connecting everyone. All our hearts and minds and shared destiny. I might just have a chance. New Orleans might not fall into the ocean and the baby blue birds might still sing their sweet melodies.

I wake up in the middle of the night damp with sweat and a dull ache behind my eyes. I'm panting. A dream. Damnit. I struggle to normalize my breathing and grab my journal from my nightstand. I write down everything that I might need to remember.

My school is on fire. It's burning to the ground. Kids are screaming and running in every direction. No one remembers all the fire drills we've practiced since kindergarten. It's a total shit show. In the back of the school near the gym, the fire starts. It's in some sort of old boiler room. The air is completely black and oily at the origin of the fire. It's chemical looking and smelling. Principal Aguilera is on the PA system trying to calm everyone down. He's telling them to go to the emergency meet up points. No one is listening. There's so much crying and screaming. The smell of burning flesh mixed with the rancid smell of unnatural elements fills our nostrils and makes it hard to breathe. I can't find Connelly. I'm searching for her every-where. Where is she? I need to find her. We need to be together. The wailing of sirens is obtrusively loud and drowns out the screams of my classmates.

It's not a Big One, but definitely still precognitive. I don't need any more distraction or responsibility right now. This is one more thing for me to have to figure out. I lay back down and kick my legs hard into my bed. I don't know why this al-ways makes me feel a little bit better but it does. I follow my legs with the thrashing if my arms against my comforter. I need to go back to sleep. It's 2:00 in the morning. I toss and turn and overthink. I lay there for hours thinking about my dreams, my plans for Queen Canary and the President, my lackluster love life, and the mountain of homework I've been ignoring. I think I fall asleep again around 4:00. I get a couple of hours in before my alarm goes off so I can do it all over again. Thank god I have ther-apy on Fridays.

CHAPTER TEN

Friday, September 13

G oing to school on Friday the 13th for someone as superstitious as me is not an easy task. I try to convince my
parents that I should stay at home and they say forget it.
Going to school on Friday the 13th *and* the day after you dream
the school burns to the ground is next level stressful. I'm jittery
with anxiety as I get ready for school. I can't even begin to deal
with my dumb layers or lip-gloss. I can't just go to school and
not do anything about my dream. I have to do something even if
it is a little thing. I can't have the burning flesh of my classmates
on the list of things the Guilt Dragon tortures me over.

I decide to leave earlier, feigning a study group for pre-cal
to appease my parents. I get to campus before too many other
people. As I make my way out near the gym where the old building sits, I see the fall sports teams practicing. Since there are so
many and not enough spaces to practice, they alternate morning and afternoon practices. Sounds terrible to me. Who wants
to lift weights at 5:30 AM? I go to the boiler room I saw in my
dream and leave a note on the door. I'm not sure what else to do,
and I have to do something.

Please inspect this room for fire hazards. I've been informed there is immediate danger.

It's enough for now. I'll talk about it more with Dr. A this afternoon. When I turn around, the soccer team is running laps around the gym and through the campus. They are right in front of the old boiler building. They are watching me watch them. Fuck. Langdon's eyes meet mine. He shoots me the middle finger. What is his deal? An involuntary shudder ripples through my body. I have a bad feeling about him.

At therapy with Dr. A, I tell her everything from last night's dream. I describe seeing my school catch fire and burn to the ground. Then I tell her about the September 11 news segment. She encourages me to not read too much into one observation regarding the President and Mr. Carpenter, but also tells me to honor my instinct. She tells me to look for more data. We talk about the power of hope and how sometimes that little winged feeling is all you need to keep going. She asks me about talking to my mom and dad about my dreams and plans. She pushes on the fact that I had another dream. Now that's two I need to tell them about. I don't have a good answer for her. I'm not sure why I haven't. I know they will be supportive. Maybe I just don't want to worry them, or maybe I have some quiet fears that I don't want to recognize. She asks me what I'm going to do about the school dream. I tell her about the note and seeing Langdon. We talk that through. She explains to me that he is likely feeling the pain of a bruised ego. She says that guys like him, the ones that seem to have it all, sometimes doesn't know how to accept being told no. She assures me that I haven't done anything wrong and that his reactions are about him and not me. That is nice to hear. It makes me feel better, but he still gives me an uneasy feeling in my belly.

We talk through my emotions, and I promise Dr. Ambrossini that I will tell my parents over the weekend, for better or for worse. She reminds me to take my medication. She checks in to see how it is making me feel. I don't love all the side-effects, but I love not feeling like I'm weighted down by lead balloons tacked all over my body, so I tell her it's fine.

I eat dinner with Connelly and Mr. Carpenter. Thankfully, Connelly asks her dad about his new job and I don't have to be a creeper again. He seems a lot more cheerful than he was last week. He describes meeting her at the Pentagon event. I don't say anything about what I saw on TV. He goes on to tell us that he makes a quick introduction of himself as she left the podium after her speech. He says that he told her to look behind her one last time because there's no going back from here on out. He continues talking and tells us that she found him at the event demanding an explanation for what he said near the podium. Connelly and I are frozen. I am especially worried about what he said and why. He goes on. I officially introduce myself to her and tell her I am her new Administrator of the EPA. She says she knows that already. She's fully aware of who I am and that she has hand selected me for the role. I told her then that she must know where I stand on the issues, and that I am going to fight hard for us to go forward because there is no going back. We are at a threshold. I let her know that I'm here to defend earth and all her inhabitants and I won't let anyone get in my way. Our jaws drop.

"DADDY! You're going to get fired before you event get started. Why would you say those things to her?" Connelly is freaking out. He interrupts her before she loses it completely.

"What will be will be, Connelly. If I've learned anything in this life, it is that you have one shot at it. I don't have anything to lose. I've already lost...," his voice fades. He seems to be about to say that he's lost everything but realizes that he hasn't. He's lost Mrs. Carpenter but not Connelly. He continues, "I've lost the love of my life. The person in this world that I was put here to love and cherish and befriend and encourage and believe in. The person I was meant to spend Saturday nights out dancing with and Sunday mornings sleeping in with. The person who I was my whole self with. She's gone. Taken from this earth by the one thing I'm supposed to protect. If that isn't a kick in the nuts, I don't know what is. Sorry, girls." He is sheepish. He takes a breath to calm down. "Now, all I have is you Connelly, and if I don't fight tooth and nail for this planet then I will have let you down too. All of this will be for nothing. Every tear I shed for your mother. Every miserable, sleepless, and lonely night. Every morning that I've woken up and forgotten for just a second that she's gone. How happy I am in that one second thinking of everything I have to be grateful for and have to look forward to. Then the next second a crashing, suffocating emptiness pressing down on my chest. Holding me down and back as I remember that she's not here. She's gone forever. She's just a shortened lifetime of memories. I'm just now returning from my darkest days. The past few months have been bearable. You've made them easier, Connelly. You make life easy. I'm back now. I'm going to complete my life's mission. I respect the Madame President. She's done a lot of good for a lot of people. Her healthcare plan allowed me to worry about one less thing when your mother was dying. But, she's wrong. I am not afraid to tell her that. I will keep telling her that until she hears me."

He finally stops talking. This is the most I've ever head Mr. Carpenter say. He looks frenzied: he's full of equal parts passion and angst. He needs for us to say something. I glance at Connelly. She is in shock. She has tears rolling down her pink, round cheeks. I reach for her hand. This is apparently the most he's ever said to her too. I break the silence. Like Mr. Carpenter said, we only have one shot. I have a mission too. I have to take every chance I can get.

"Mr. Carpenter, we are on your side. We support you. It seems like you have a big job to do, but it also sounds like you're, like, really ready. Really prepared. Very passionate." I keep going. I don't want to be stopped. "I think you're right about the President too. She seems like she just needs the right person do to give her the truth, just like you're doing. I know you can do it. Maybe if you're just like, you know, nice to her and respectful. Maybe do some sweet things for her or something like that. You know to let her know that you think she's doing a good job and stuff. You could write her a note or bring her some chocolates or flowers. Sweet things like that. I think, maybe, Mrs. Carpenter would want to you too."

Oh shit. I did it. I went there. I might have gone too far. I look up to see how my last sentences impacts both of them. Neither one of them seem to be fully present. Each lost in their own little worlds of memories for a few seconds. He's in a trance. He comes back to us. "Thank you, Simone. Thank you for saying that. It's a hard job, but I'm up for it. I'm already making progress with the President. I'm going to keep at it. Girls, why don't you finish your dinner on your own and enjoy some time without your old dad around. I'm going to go for a walk." He leaves us in the kitchen and heads for the front door. "Connelly," I say. "Are you okay?" She's still quiet but not as stunned.

"I think so. I just haven't heard my dad talk about my mom like that in a long time. For awhile, it was like she never existed. I miss her a lot. I know he does too, but it's like we've been ignoring the fact that she's not here. But I've been needing him to say something. Anything. I've felt kind of alone. I don't care what he does at work. Basically, I don't even understand anything that he does. I just want him to be happy. Even though he seems kind of mad right now, it's better than him acting like he feels nothing at all."

I stretch my neck from side to side and breathe in for four long ones and out for five longer ones. This evening is wearing me out. "The Babysitters Club" is sounding better and better right now. We haven't even left for the game and my "date" yet. I groan with apprehension. I check the Yabo app hoping that Stephen has cancelled so that we can just stay home and have a Netflix and popcorn binge instead. He has sent me a pic of him at the stadium doing his band warm ups. The picture is a tightly cropped selfie. His face taking up the whole frame. A bit of the bleachers and green field in the background. His face is covered in a film of sweat. A few red, shiny, unapologetic pimples dot his cheeks. His instrument held closely to his face. It's fine. It's going to be fine. At least he seems like a pleasant person and not a racist ass hole, so that's good. I refocus my attention on Connelly.

"Connelly, I'm sorry you feel alone. I wish I could make you feel better. I can't imagine what you're going through. I'm sorry if I've been a bad friend." She cuts me off and tells me that she never feels alone when she's with Zach. She tries to include being with me too at the end of her statement, but it falls a little flat. I don't take offense, not too much. What Connelly has going on is bigger than me. I wish she would go see Dr. A. I think it would help her a lot. It's helps me every single week. My therapy with her is mission critical to my life. We sit in silence for a few moments. She says we need to hurry up and finish eating, so that we can go get ready. We can't go looking like we came straight from school. I don't know why we can't, but she assures me that would be unacceptable. This Friday the 13th is shaping up to be quite a day. We still have the game and The Jukebox to go.

We finish our food and head upstairs to "freshen up." Connelly takes her time with my hair and make-up and does a good job recreating Tiffany's work. I am over done for football, I think, but she assures me that this is what all the girls do. Seems like a big waste of time to me. Her dad takes us to the game. He's composed himself and no one says anything else about the dinner conversation. He's back to his cheerful self, telling dad jokes and warning us to be careful. He'll pick us up at The Jukebox at 10:30. Wow. Late night. The game is fine. I don't know much about football, but our friends are there. I watch the cheerleaders with more interest than I do the football team. I don't understand them. What are they doing? Why? What is the point of them? They look cute though, I'll give them that. Very Connelly in their put together hair and make-up. Very toned and confident in their bodies' movements. Their smiles competing with the shine of the field's massive lights. I'm fascinated. I get a lot of compliments on my hair cut. That's good I guess.

After the game, Zach drives us to The Jukebox to meet Stephen. He's already there. He's sitting by himself in a corner booth even though the place is packed with students and their parents. Parents sitting under a huge red model Corvette hanging from the ceiling over the bar. The kids piled two and three to a seat around the perimeter of the restaurant. Except for Stephen. Just one at his table. We approach him and he gives a silent wave. No smile. Not like the pic he sent before the game. Now it looks like his face is hurting him. He's still visibly sweating though. Zach and Connelly walk us to his table and introduce themselves. When Connelly explains that she's Khalil's cousin, a flicker of curious confusion crosses Stephen's face, but at least he doesn't make any ignorant comments. I sit down across from him, but Connelly and Zach remain standing. Then they ghost us. No explanation, they just disappear.

Now it's just me and him. It's immediately clear that when you put two awkward people together for an awkward first date, it's a super awkward conversation. I ask him a few questions and he literally says nothing. I bring up his band friends that we messaged about hoping this will make him more comfortable. He just nods or shakes his head when I ask him questions. He looks like he wants to talk but can't. My god. I keep looking around for Connelly and Zach but never spot them. Where are they? What are they even doing?

I order a hot fudge brownie sundae for something to do. His face lights up and we only talk about the sundae for the remaining duration of the date. At least we have that in common. I love a good sundae, but there's only so much you can say about one for 45 minutes. I like cherries. I like cherries too. I like when the brownie is warm, but not too hot because then the ice cream melts too fast. Yeah, me too. I like vanilla ice cream with a chocolate brownie. It balances everything out. Me too. Hate nuts. Love nuts. Wow, this ice cream is cold and delicious. You're right. It is cold and delicious. It's a very long 45 minutes.

I'm so tempted to pull out my phone and check my

Queen Canary accounts. I feel like I'm wasting time. Stephen is nice but awkward as hell. I don't think I can find true love with someone who can only talk about dessert. Or can I? Maybe that is the secret to a successful relationship. No, no it is not. Don't be silly. Stephen is not my guy. I feel bad for him but not bad enough to do this again. I also realize sitting next to him that I'm probably six inches taller than him. That is not okay. Not in tenth grade. The pull of Queen Canary is almost too much to resist. I need a distraction from this sad little date.

This week I found a website that puts out a picture of day of climate devastation. Anyone can use them to raise awareness. I've been posting them with facts and comments and they are going gangbusters. My following is huge. Mr. Carpenter is right; we are at a tipping point. People are ready for change. I resist the urge to pull out my phone. Finally, Connelly and Zach reappear. Mr. Carpenter will be here any minute. I say bye to Stephen. That's literally all I say. Bye. He waves half-heartedly. Good grief.

We move towards the door and low and behold, in walks Langdon Harris. Shit. He fist bumps Zach and puts his arm out to block me as I walk by. "Thought you couldn't come out tonight because of your family French fries or whatever."

"Changed my mind." I keep walking and he grabs at my wrist with his outstretched arm. "you're a little psychotic witch," he whispers through gritted teeth and smiling mouth. Jesus. I don't say anything. He must have heard the rumors about my dreams and me and after seeing me this morning put two and two together or made some crazy assumption about what he saw. I hate him. He releases my wrist and I hurry up and out the door. Tears sting my eyes. I squeeze them shut. In for four, out for five. I don't think anyone else heard him. Thank god. I'm already hot with embarrassment. Beads of sweat sit on the skin above my lip. I can't believe how hurt my feelings are. What the hell is wrong with him? Screw Friday the 13th and screw him.

CHAPTER ELEVEN

Saturday September 14

I spend Saturday morning in bed doing research and working on my plans. In my journal, I take inventory of my progress.

My Quest for True Love

1. Horrible date with ignorant, mean Langdon
2. Awkward as hell date with silent Stephen
3. Pissed off Langdon and now I'm a psychotic witch (apparently)
4. Had a makeover that I hate
5. Miss my long hair and braid
6. Kind of like the lip gloss tho
7. Have a dating profile that looks nothing like me

Get the President of the United States of America to Find True Love

1. Told Mr. Carpenter to be nice to her
2. Said she was pretty
3. Encouraged Mr. Carpenter to get to know her
4. This list is short and I'm never going to complete my mission

To Do This Week

1. Schedule another soul sucking date from Yubo
2. Learn to fix my layers

3. Get a date for Homecoming, try to love him
4. Get Connelly onboard with plan
5. I have no ideas
6. This is a stupid plan
7. It's never going to work
8. We are doomed

I drop my journal in defeat and pick up my phone. I check Twitter. I scroll through #climatecrisis. There's a lot going on. I retweet a bunch of stuff from the @queencanary account which has 17,000 followers now. I have like 74 on my personal account. I guess people aren't that hyped on seeing pictures of Cherry Garcia, an old ugly Pug who hates having his picture taken. I'm getting ready to post a new picture of a woman riding a bike through lanes and lanes of bumper to bumper traffic. There are plumes of black, sooty smoke in the background. I'm going to caption it with something about how we need better bike infrastructure to make it easier for people to choose clean, green transportation. I also pat myself on the back for walking to school. Good job, Simone! While I'm working on the post, I get a notification from @undercoverearthmom1965. It says: *what r u going to do about this?* She includes a link to a classified report that lists out hundreds of environmental and health issues at schools across the country. Oh shit.

I scan the report and my eyes get stuck on some bad stuff. Students are experiencing problems with contaminated water, poor air quality, radioactivity, and toxic foods grown or manufactured with chemicals. The report outlines a conspiracy to further the divide between the advantaged and disadvantaged schools. The advantaged schools have *way* more resources and access to services and products that can reduce the negative impact of the environmental problems occurring at their schools. The government is making a ton of money off the schools as they buy all that stuff to counteract the problems. But, the schools that don't have the extra financial resources to combat the problems at the school, continue to have them. Their students are getting sick and even dying from environmental related illnesses. Also the low-income schools can't counteract the environmental issues and then their old schools add to the issues of the climate crisis. The school buildings emit tons of poisonous gasses into the atmosphere which over warms their communities, which then makes their whole community at risk.

It's a viscous cycle. If you're in a "rich" school, you have the issues and the government doesn't care. They want you to have the issues so they can make their money. If you're a "poor" school, then you can't keep your students well, you can't fix your school, and your school adds to unnatural climate change in your community. Then they are blamed and considered part of the problem. The government punishes you when the sick students aren't successful on standardized testing and things like that. Then you lose funding that you need to make the school a healthier place. A healthier school would equal healthier students. Healthier students would mean better test scores. Better test scores would mean more money for the school but less money for the government. Greedy, greedy, greedy.

The government is actively participating in the segregation of resources. They are intentionally separating the poor and the rich. They aren't helping the planet and they aren't helping students. They are financially gaining from making the earth and the students sick. I move my phone away from my face. Geeezus. Why did I get this? Who is @undercoverearthmom1965? What am I supposed to do with this? My heart is racing. There's a stream of sweat snaking down my back. I know one thing. I'm pissed and I'm scared. I've seen first-hand what happens when the environment makes people sick. They die.

I start researching the report's facts. I validate most of the report from other reliable resources. The part I don't confirm is probably what makes this document classified: the conspiracy. *Shitballs.* This is huge. This is serious. I pace around my room. My chest tightens and it's hard for me to breathe. I can't get a full breath. I feel the information and the responsibility closing in on me. I think about Dr. A and what she would say. She's the one who encouraged me to start running as part of my wellness protocol that we came up with after I overdosed. I need to get out of the house. I need to move my body. I need to remove myself from the trigger. I grab my shoes, a hair-tie, put on my sports bra, and go for a run.

I run my usual route and stop at Khalil's like I normally do. His dad answers the door. No power suit today. Baggy gray sweatpants and a Harvard Law School t-shirt. He says Khalil's out. He doesn't say where. I ask if he's at the gym, but his dad says no and leaves it at that. We talk for a few minutes about the weather and Connelly. I'm distracted and disappointed Khalil's not home. He's the only person I can talk to about all of this. The love part, the science part, the President part. Mr. Williams is asking me what I think about Zach. I collect my wandering thoughts. I'm not sure what to say. I realize I don't really know much about Zach. That in itself is odd. He nods his head and says he understands. He mentions Khalil's continued interest in his science project. I swear he's looking at me like he knows more than he's letting on. Another one of those "knowing looks" that adults are so good at. Admittedly, I'm probably a little paranoid. I agree. He's really focusing in on that schoolwork. Before it gets weird, I say I have to go. I sprint the rest of the way home. My arms, legs, and blood pumping to the rhythm of my racing mind.

When I get back, my head is clear. I pull out my phone. I think about the past few weeks and everything that has happened. All that I've learned. I know that the world is in bad, bad shape. I have a dream that shows the future if we don't change the way we live. The vision of the future plus all the research I've done to better understand why we are in the position we are in, leads me to believe that the time is **now**. The proof is everywhere. It's with the experts like Mr. Carpenter. It's in books and articles and websites. It's in classified reports. Honestly, it doesn't take someone with my gift, freaky as it may be, to see the future. What I have that no one else does though is a divine answer. My answer came from the universe, from the beyond. That's where crystal clear and untethered truth is. True love. Find true love. I have the answer given to me by the gods and goddesses, by the love of a mother, a dead mother at that, and the omniscience of the universe. I have to stay the course on all aspects of my plan. I can't give up on dating. In fact, I need to turn it up a notch. I won't give up on it even though I might actually hate it.

I don't feel like I'm doing enough about the President situation though. When I really think about how impossible this mission sounds, I am big time anxious. What can I really do about her falling in love? It's impossible for me to do something about that. I also know that now I know too much. In addition to what I know from Tyler Anderson, The East Coast Medium, I also have the classified information. I can't let that go. For some reason, I've also been chosen to see that.

I'm learning that a lot of people know a lot of shit about the climate crisis and they aren't doing a thing about it. I need a full court press to inspire change. From what I can tell, it's up to each of us to do our part to restore the Earth to her normal patterns. I need to be different. Connelly needs to be different. My school needs to be different. Even Mr. Carpenter has to change. The President has to do her part. We all have to contribute. With all I have on my plate, I have to get serious about my own resistance, my own rebellion against the status quo. I'm going to do my part and lead a revolution. My tweets aren't enough. I need action. Big, meaningful action.

I send a message to @undercoverearthmom1965. *Got your link. Why me?* I want to explain my dream and tell her just how scared but determined I am. I don't want to freak her out though. I wait for a moment and then grab my journal as I wait for her response. I look back at the list I made earlier and add to it.

To Do This Week

1. Schedule another soul sucking date from yubo
2. Learn to fix my layers
3. Get a date for Homecoming, try to fall in love with him fast
4. Get Connelly onboard
5. ~~I have no ideas~~
6. ~~This is a stupid plan~~
7. ~~It's never going to work~~
8. Tell mom and dad everything
9. Start a revolution
10. Don't give up

My phone chirps. I pick it up and there's a message from @undercoverearthmom1965. *ur the chosen one.* I am chosen to do this work. I know the future. I know the answer. The universe is knowledge and love and perfection. I've heard from the other side. I carry the torch. I'm anxious and empowered. I am chosen. I am chosen. I am chosen. I choose. I need to lead by example. I keep writing in my journal.

What I Can Do

1. Eat plants
2. No more single use plastics
3. Buy less, only what I need
4. Create less waste
5. Compost
6. Keep learning and changing
7. Get mom and dad to change over to low flow, LED, etc.
8. Find out if my school is on the classified report and fix it
9. Protest the government's current stance on climate science
10. Expose the conspiracy
11. Become a movement

This might be a lot to take on right away, but it has to be

done. There's no reason I can't do it. It won't be easy and I'll need help, but I have no choice. I go downstairs to cross the first thing off my list. My mom and dad are sitting at the kitchen table still drinking coffee and reading the paper. "I need to talk." My mom lays the paper down on top of her phone with an intentional thud. I notice she catches my dad's eye. "Talk to us, Queen Canary."

I lay it all out there. I tell them everything about my dreams and Tyler Anderson, The East Coast Medium. They aren't thrilled with me for going to the conference without them knowing, but I talk fast and keep going when they try to cut in. I tell them what the medium told me about true love. I tell them about the hours of research that I've done. I tell them about @queencanary and all the followers who now call themselves The Flock. I tell them about the classified report. I tell them that I am so overwhelmed because I need to do so many things. It's up to me. I talk until I'm out of breath. My parents wait for me to finish.

"Your mother and I believe in you, Simone. We've always trusted your gift. And you're right. The climate crisis is a real and pressing issue. But, sweetheart, it isn't your problem to figure out. While I trust your dream, I'm not sure I trust the wisdom and advice you received from the Sixth Sense Conference. Your mother and I are long-term supporters of taking care of the Earth. Maybe we haven't done enough, though. I see that now. We will help you with parts of your mission, but I don't think we can support all of the many pieces you have listed. For one thing, it is not our place to meddle in someone's love life. Plus, I just can't come up with any realistic ideas for how that would even work. We don't even know the President. You and Mr. Carpenter are right though. She needs to believe in the science. She's wields the power to create systemic change." I try to butt in and remind them about Mr. Carpenter's new job and how he like actually knows her now, but they aren't having it. My dad keeps going.

"There is a lot that you can do. There's a lot that each of us can do. We are with you in figuring out what you want to focus on and helping you see that plan through. I need to see this classified report. I'm still not quite sure how or why you got that. Maybe that's where you focus your efforts. Simone, we think you can do whatever you set your mind to. If you want to save the world, let's do it. We're behind you."

My mom hasn't said anything yet. I look at her. I'm not sure what she's thinking. She opens her mouth to say something but doesn't. "Mom, I'm sorry I didn't tell you sooner. I just, I wanted to have a plan. I didn't want you to worry." She is teary. "I'm proud of you Simone Alice Marker." That's all she says, then she gets up and leaves the room. My dad watches her go. No emotion on his face. He picks up where he left off. "Send me the report. Figure out a focused plan. Come back and ask for the help you need." I go back to my room and look at my list again. I make some notes.

<u>What I Can Do</u>

1. Eat plants-already started, keep doing it, just need to make sure mom and dad are onboard-try and get some more vegan and plant based foods at school??? May need help.
2. No more single use plastics-easy enough, right? will do it, don't need help.
3. Buy less, only what I need-easy, barely have any money to begin with, ask mom and dad for less, don't need help.
4. Create less waste-can do this alone, don't need help.
5. Compost-will ask mom and dad to get that going at home, it sounds kind of gross tho.
6. Keep learning-keep doing my research every day, can't get enough, must know the facts.
7. Get mom and dad to change over to low flow, LED, etc-easy, just give them the research and ask them to do it.
8. Tell mom and dad everything-didn't go exactly how I thought, but good enough.

9. Protest the government's current stance on climate science – need people, need help.
10. Expose the conspiracy-no idea what to do, need help.
11. Become a movement.

When I get to the last one, I pause. I remember learning something about movements, but I can't think of the specifics. I chew on the end of my pen for a moment. Then it comes to me; it was a lesson from my world history class. Maybe I've been paying more attention that I give myself credit for. I reach for my history folder and thumb through my notes until I find the section I'm looking for. I scan the pages and then I see this quote.

Bill McKibben-"Movements take 5-10 percent of people and make them decisive—because in a world where apathy rules, 5-10 percent is an enormous number."

I look up the word apathy to make sure I know what it means: indifference, lazy, doing nothing. So, I think what McKibben is saying is that once you have 5-10 percent of people doing something different or doing something about a problem, then you have a chance at change. You have a movement not just an idea or a little pocket of absurd people. I think about the people protesting on the mall the day of the wrestling tournament. They are a movement. They are thousands of people doing something about what they believe in. I remember thinking that they looked brave, confident, united, passionate, and unstoppable. I want to start a movement. I want to be a movement. I want to start a movement at my school and in Longview and in D.C. I keep saying and thinking that I want to have this kind of impact, but I'm not really doing anything about it besides my socials. I pull up the classified report again and make some notes about the conspiracy in my journal. I can do better.

The Conspiracy Summarized

The government is intentionally exacerbating climate change by not investing in schools that are making kids and the earth sick. They profit off the wealthy schools that can pay to fix their own prob-

lems while protecting the rich kids. The poor schools are in a vicious cycle. Their schools have environmental problems. The problems make their students and communities sick. The buildings themselves are adding dangerous gasses and chemicals to the whole town. Then their students don't perform well and they lose funding. Funding goes only to the rich schools. Then they spend it to solve their problems. The government gets more money.

I wonder if President Robinson is in on this. What if she doesn't want to be but she's forced to? What if she doesn't know at all? What if she's being threatened? What if she knows but doesn't know how to make it right? What if she believes in the conspiracy and wants it to happen? I have no way of knowing right now. I know what I need to do. I go downstairs to talk to my dad. I see he's moved to the garage. He's getting ready to do his Saturday chores.

I'm breathless when I find him. "Dad, I know what I need to do. I have a focused plan like you said, and I forwarded you the link to the classified report. I know this sounds kind of nuts, but I want to lead a movement to reveal the school conspiracy that's described in the report. Well, that's part of what I want to do. There's more. I know you don't exactly believe in what the medium said, but I can't take a chance. I have to keep searching for true love and I have to figure out how to get the President to also. Please don't be mad. I just have to. In the meantime, I know that I can't just sit on the information that's been given to me. I just need to do both. I'm sorry. I know you think I'm silly, but I can't risk it. I have to do everything that I can. I can't handle any more blood on my hands. No more guilt." The Guilt Dragon raises its hungry head at the sound of its name. My voice cracks and it's hard to keep talking. My dad shakes his head sadly. He hates that I feel so guilty about Mrs. Carpenter. "I need to start today. I need your help."

My dad steps towards me and bear hugs me. He's a big man, tall with leftover muscles from when he was younger. Now padded by ice cream that we share straight from the carton even though mom yells at us. We talk about the help I need and he assures me he's on it. He abandons his lawnmower and we go inside to get started.

CHAPTER TWELVE

Monday, September 16

A t school on Monday, I try to act normal or at least as normal as I ever act. I am nervous though. I have a lot to do this week. First up is asking someone to the Homecoming dance. I can't sit around and wait for some dude to ask me out. I need love and I need it fast. Connelly is waiting for me at my locker as usual. No muffin. We catch up on the weekend. She and Zach had a date on Saturday night and hung out all day on Sunday. I was so caught up planning with my mom and dad that I didn't realize I hadn't heard from her. What a good friend I am. I bring up Homecoming because I know she's into it. I didn't go last year, but this year it seems like a good excuse for a date. It's at least something to do that warrants going somewhere with a boy. Connelly is not thrilled about me asking a boy out. I don't see how it is any different than blasting my makeover pics on Snapchat, but what do I know?

We brainstorm some options. We both agree that sophomore boys are well, sophomoric, so we consider Zach's friends. He's a junior. I don't actually know that junior boys are any more mature but I'm hopeful. She texts Zach to ask him for some recommendations. He texts back and suggests Axl James. He says Axl asked about me last week when he saw me at school on Thursday. It's not lost on me that Thursday is the day that Connelly fixed my hair and make-up since she slept over on Wednesday night. I hope he doesn't see me today if that's what he's expecting. This morning, I was working on my plan and posting a bunch of climate stuff on my socials. I barely had time to even take a shower.

By lunchtime, it's agreed that Axl and I will go to the homecoming dance with Connelly and Zach. I get out of having to straight up ask him myself which I'm relieved about. Apparently I have to get a fancy-ish dress. Connelly agrees to help. Thank god. We make a plan to go shopping on Wednesday. We have a half day. She tries to make me get an appointment with Tiffany, but I refuse. She says she can do my hair. I just have to get to her house early so we have enough time. I can't imagine how much time she's going to need. I'm already antsy just thinking about it. The rest of the day goes by fast. We're at that point in the school year where we are finished reviewing all the things that we forgot from last year and are starting to get into new stuff. I need to pay attention, and it's difficult with all that I have going on in my head. I'm distracted. Honestly though, will it really matter if know anything about Mesopotamia if the world overheats and we all die? So, I give myself a break when my mind wanders or when I sneak in @queencanary Twitter posts during long lectures on the root of a polynomial or the hero's journey. I have my own hero's journey to live.

After I half-ass my homework, I look back at the plan my dad and I worked on. There are two main things I need to do this week. The first one is to write up a scathing poster about the school conspiracy and post them all over my town. Yep, my school was right there on the list like thousands of others. I'm starting to wonder if the dream I had about the fire at my school has something to do with the report. I'm hopeful it was just symbolic and not something that really happens. I haven't heard or seen anything in response to the note I left on the boiler room door. Normally I'm happy about that but not right now. All Saints is not on the list, but their school is so close to

ours. They need to know what's happening. If our school building is contributing to our local climate change, it's affecting
them too. Plus I just hope they have the decency to care.. I create
a different flyer to post at All Saints. I'm going to wallpaper our
town with them. I text Khalil to see if he'll help.

hey

sup sis

i'm not your sis

i need ur help w queen canary

see what i can do

i have some flyers i need u 2 post @ all saints

like everywhere

i'll make copies and leave them at ur house tomorrow

what r they about

you'll see

check queen canary accounts on thurs

will post something big

k sis

count on us

That's the second thing I need to do. I'm going to post a
summary of the classified report and a link to it. I'm going to tag
everyone I can think of that should know about it. I'm going to
ask The Flock to share it and make sure it goes viral. I'm starting a movement. A big one. I pinch myself. It feels amazing to
do something good for a change. I feel like I'm finally making
up for the bad things I've done. Mrs. Carpenter. Hurting myself.
I try not to think about that night too often. I'm so ashamed
that I did that to myself, to my parents, to Connelly, to Cherry
Garcia. It's so embarrassing. Dr. A and my parents assure me that

it wasn't me entirely. It's part of the sickness that I have. That's why I have to take care of myself. Go to therapy. Run. Talk. Breathe. And now Project Queen Canary. It's part of my healing, of getting and staying well.

I spend the next hour before bed making my flyer. I send it to my dad and ask him to make copies at work. He replies back with a series of emojis that make no sense, but they have a generally happy vibe to them, so I think he's agreeing. A simple yes would do it, Dad.

disillusionment is a form of heartache

everyup always distd heart

CHAPTER THIRTEEN

Wednesday, September 18

W ell before dawn, my mom and dad go with me to post the flyers all over town. We drop a big stack off at Khalil's house. He's going to go to school early to post them for me before the other kids get to campus. He gets up early to work out before school anyways, so it's not a big deal to him. He's crazy, but he's ripped. I'll give him that.

On the way to school on Wednesday, I get a text and pics from Khalil.

mission accomplished sis

thanks

ur a good friend

looks like some serious shit

more info tmrw?

yeah, check it out

its bad

but we can fix it

i have 2 believe that

word

I'm grateful to Khalil. He is a good friend. I'm lucky to have him even if he is annoying. I can't wait to get to school. I don't want to be the first one there though. I don't want look suspicious. I wait and leave at the same time I normally do. When I get there, the school is alive. It is buzzing. It's a hive of activity, movement, and sound. Buzzzzzzz. Everyone is pissed. Everyone is huddled together talking loudly and asking each other questions about what the flyer *really* means. Teachers are standing in pairs, shaking their heads. There are some tears. There are raised voices. Lockers slam. Emotion pulses through the hallways and spills out into the courtyards, atriums, and athletic fields. The whole school is tense.

Connelly is at my locker with a flyer in hand. She's reading it intently. She doesn't look like her usual jolly self. Without a hello she says, "Do you think this is why mom got sick? Because she spent so many years at this school? First as a student and then as a teacher? Do you think they made her sick? On purpose?"

Connelly is pissed. She's so hurt and angry. She's like a little baby volcano that has been building up to this moment and she's about to erupt. I hadn't really put two and two together like that. But yes, it makes perfect sense. How did I miss that? Of course Connelly would see the connection instantly, and unfortunately the answer is yes, I think. I hate to see Connelly upset. I hate to be the one to make her upset. It hurts me to hurt my friend that I love like my very own sister. I also have to act like I don't know what she's talking about yet. She doesn't know about @queencanary. Why haven't I talked to her about this yet? I need her help. I hate these decisive secrets. A wave of regret crashes over me. Guilt Dragon. I hate lying to my best friend. We are better together.

"What are you talking about, Con? What's going on?" I reach in to hug her, to calm her down. Tame the impending eruption. It's hot and gurgling. She pushes the flyer into my hands. I inspect it like I don't know it backward and forwards, like I didn't pour my heart and soul into it. For Connelly. For Mrs. Carpenter. For all of us. To defeat the Guilt Dragon. I take this time to think about what I should say. I breathe.

"Yeah, from what I'm seeing here. Yes, it looks like whatever this conspiracy thing is, it made your mom sick." I look her in the eye, and I just keep lying. Why don't I just tell her the truth? Why don't I just tell her about @queencanary? Why don't I remind her about my dream and my plans? Why don't I ask her to help me? Instead I say, "I'm sorry about your mom, Connelly. I'm so, so, so sorry. You of all people don't deserve what happened to you." This is probably the one-millionth time that I've said something like this to her. Connelly starts to cry. Plump, silent tears. Fat, little diamonds. Heavy. Her chest moves up and down faster and harder than it should. I just hug her. I don't know what else to do. We stand that way, hugging. I'm going to tell her everything. My plans. Her mom's message. How I need her. I open my mouth to backtrack. To undo the damage I've done to our friendship. Damage that she doesn't even know exists. "Connelly, I need to tell you…" The loud speaker interrupts the start of my confession.

"Students…students, please be quiet and listen up for a few moments. This is Principal Aguilera. Listen up students. This is very important. It is clear that whomever posted these flyers around the school today wants to send us a message. They clearly want to scare us and disrupt the rigorous learning that we have planned for today. At this time, there is no proof, I repeat, there is no proof, that the flyers reflect anything proven or factual. Please don't panic or get upset. I will investigate this further throughout the day and report back to you when I know more. In advance, I thank you for staying calm and staying focused on your studies. We have many important things to learn today. Also, I need your help in figuring out who posted these flyers. This is grounds for inciting a riot. Boys and girls, we can't just go around making incendiary comments. Not on school property. If you know anything about the instigator, please come by my office and let's talk. You know I'm here for you, students. Okay, Lions, thank you for your attention and let's make it another great day at Longview High."

Seriously every single student around me moans in exasperation at the end of Principal Aguilera's announcement. He is so lame. I on the other hand felt a surge of panic. I hadn't thought about getting in trouble for posting the flyers. Mom and Dad mentioned it but seemed willing to take the risk, all things considered. I thought they were overreacting. I text my dad and tell him about Principal Aguilera's announcement. He says not to worry. He's got my back.

It's time to go to first block. I squeeze Connelly's arm. "I love you, Connelly. You're my best friend. I hate when you're sad. I wish I could make it all better." I am doing what I can to make it better. To make up for what I didn't do before and now to make it so that no one else gets sick and the earth gets better too. I really am doing all I can. I can't tell her this yet, but I realize now that I have to tell her and I have to do it soon.

Connelly's dad picks us up from school and we take the train together to D.C. We don't talk about the morning's events. I know Connelly doesn't want to upset her dad. I haven't released the report online yet. Connelly is back to all bubbles and rainbows and butterflies. All hearts and light. It's impressive if I do say so myself, and also a little scary.

Connelly assures me the only place to get a homecoming dress is at the Rent the Runway storefront in Georgetown. She has a list of other high-end boutiques that we have to window shop first to get ideas. Blah. She actually has a mini clipboard with her lists. *A clipboard.* Lists of the places we need to go to and lists the things we need to get. Lord have mercy.

As we get close to the city, Mr. Carpenter casually asks us if we want a tour of his office… at The White House. I stare at him in shock. Connelly cocks her head like Cherry Garcia but doesn't say anything right away. We're waiting for the punchline. "Are you serious, Mr. Carpenter? Like for real? Like inside the White House?"

"Sure, why not? You're here. I have a little extra time before an important meeting this afternoon. You girls should see the inner workings of your government. I've never had access to The White House like I do with my new job. It's pretty darn tooting cool if I do say so myself. I'd like to show it off to my best girls!"

I can't believe my good luck. I give a silent shout out to the universe. This is my chance to get close to the President! Also, it's so much better than dress shopping. I glance at Connelly. Her head is still tilted to one side. She's very still and her eyes are wide. She is of course going to agree to the tours, but I also know she's calculating how much time that leaves us for Operation Homecoming Dress. She's also too nice to say anything whiny, so she smiles, nods and easily agrees. "That sounds nice, Daddy."

As I remember the horror of the school conspiracy report and the role of the government, the very same government that I'm about to see the inner workings of, my stomach churns, swirling my oatmeal around. I need to take advantage of this moment. What to do? I squeeze my eyes close for a few seconds and then do the only thing I can think of. I pull out my cross body and dig into the side pocket. There is a stack of Post-its and my journal. I pull them both out. I still the Posit-its in the journal and use it as a little shield. I furiously write as many climate crisis facts as I can and sign them @queencanary. Thankfully, Connelly is used to my scribblings and is not paying me any attention.

We make our way to the White House. It's a short walk and the day is nice. It's sunny and still warm but not hot like true summer. I am so glad that Connelly suggested I clean up a bit before we go. She says you want to look like you'll look the night you wear the dress so you can see how it all works together. I pull the cherry gloss out of my pocket and run it over my thin lips. Connelly mocks me with a shocked nod of approval and a big grin.

We enter the White House by completing a series of security tasks. I'm nervous even though I don't have anything to be nervous about. The police are also very stern and serious. Not mall cops. More like military. We make it inside and Mr. Carpenter speaks quietly with a woman who looks like she's worked at the White House since George Washington was President. She nods excitedly but it's still slow as a sloth. When he's done speaking to her, they wave for us to join them. The ancient little lady places lanyards around our necks. She says we must keep them on at all times and not give them to anyone and certainly don't lose them. They are our very special and privileged tickets to roam the house. Hardly anyone gets access like we have today. She also says don't touch anything. She wags her finger at us. I don't think she can help herself.

We are led through the White House by a large, sturdy man wearing jet black everything including sunglasses. He guides us from room to room on the main floor. He stands at the door of each room protecting us while we look around. He doesn't say anything. He lets us look and then he motions for us to move rooms. I've been to the White House before. When you live an hour away, you take a lot of field trips to the Capital. I'm still in awe of the White House though. The colors alone are breathtaking. Emerald greens, deep corals, popping blues, scarlet reds, shimmering golds. Everything in its perfect place, shining brightly. All of the beautiful colors and objects seems less shiny to me today though. I can't help but think of the conspiracy. The children. The students. The sickness. The money. The greed. The earth.

Mr. Carpenter finds us in the Library. I can't help it. I'm blatantly disobeying the little old bird of a lady from the foyer, and I'm touching the spines of the books, running my fingers along their ridges. Hoping their information will seep into my brain by osmosis. He asks how it is going. We nod. It is really cool to be roaming this gorgeous with no one breathing down our necks. It feels sacred in here, or at least it felt like it was a sacred place once upon a time. He says he has a surprise for us and motions for us to follow him.

As we move through the White House, I leave Post-its tucked clandestinely into spots I think important people might find them. When I can, I snap a quick picture of each one I leave. I'm saving one though, and I'm hopeful Mr. Carpenter is leading us to a place where I can leave it for the Madame President to find.

He is. He takes us to the Oval Office and knocks confidently on the door. Three heavy raps and a fourth light one. A woman's voice calls us in. I don't expect to be tongue-tied, but I am. I'm immediately star-struck. She's sitting at a big, glossy wooden desk writing furiously in a journal, like I do. She's smaller than I imagined. She looks propped up to fit the giant desk. Like maybe she's sitting in a booster seat. Her hair lays in a perfect angled mahogany bob with a few thin silver streaks at her temples. She's dressed in a navy blue skirted suit with pink pinstripes and an American flag broach made of rhinestones and glittering diamonds. Her skin, the color of toasted almond, is smooth and soft looking. Smile lines frame her teardrop eyes and rosebud lips. I realize I'm staring. She says something to us again. I hear her for the first time. She's laughing. "Come in, girls. Come in. It's so nice to meet you. I love having young women in the White House. Have a seat."

She leads us to a sitting area with plush couches and straight back wooden chairs. She perches on the end of one. I need to get a grip. I still haven't even said anything. Connelly isn't doing any better though. Connelly is obsessed with President Robinson. She loves her style. Her clothes. Her shoes. Her hair. Her make-up. Her jewelry. Things I never really notice until I see her now. She is breathtaking in a *no-nonsense, I'm here to run the world while looking amazing and unfuckable with* kind

of way. Finally, Connelly saves us. "Your suit. The stripes. Pink."
Okay, well *saves us* is a stretch. She sounds like she just learned
to talk yesterday.

"This old thing?" the President laughs. "A personal stylist
who gets me is one of the best things about this job. The other
stuff, well, meh." She laughs again. I can't remember ever seeing
her laugh on TV. She seems so much nicer in person. She realizes
she will have to carry this conversation, so she keeps going.
"Your dad tells me you ladies are very interested in American
and world politics, so how could I resist inviting you up?" Connelly glances at her dad and he winks. Oh my god, I hope she
doesn't ask us any questions about politics. Connelly definitely
won't know anything and well, the things I have to say are probably not going to get us invited back. "It's not an easy job, I'll
tell you that. Politics will eat you up and spit you out. You have
to have thick skin, people you trust, and fast decision-making
skills. Every day I have to make decisions that affect millions of
lives. I have to trust the information people give me and then be
okay with the decision no matter what any news outlet or Twitter or even individual citizens have to say about it. I've learned
I can't make everyone happy. I'm not a hot fudge brownie sundae." My ears perk up and *this* is what I say to the President of the
United States of America, "I love hot fudge brownie sundaes so
much." I hate myself.

The President laughs again. "They are my favorite. Now
that I think about it. There are several perks of the job. Did
you know I have a personal chef on staff? She lives here at the
White House and she makes me whatever I want when I want it.
I would eat sundaes every day, but I have to keep an eye on my
figure. The media annihilates me if I put on even five pounds. It
is preposterous. But on Sundays, Chef Bess makes me the most
delectable hot fudge brownie sundae that there ever was. I look
forward to it all week." She looks wistful. It's only Wednesday.

I can't believe we are still talking about ice cream. Who
am I? Silent Stephen? There is so much that I actually want to

say about important things, but I can't get my brain and my mouth to line up. Focus, Simone. My god. Focus. I take a long, hopefully silent breath to get oxygen to my malfunctioning brain.

With a hit of air, I'm able to formulate a thought. For some reason, I ask, "Who do you trust? I mean you mentioned you have to trust people a lot, so like, um, who do you trust the most?" She peers at me. Suddenly more serious, more like TV President than Oval Office President. "That's a thoughtful question," she says. "It depends on the topic. I have experts for different decisions that I have to make. Thankfully I have people like him," she indicates Mr. Carpenter, "who I trust based on their reputation and previous work and record. That helps. But I've made mistakes. Before I hired Mr. Carpenter, I learned that I couldn't trust some of the people who had his job before him." She looks sad. A flicker of anger quickens across her face. I start to get my shit together and feel more confident. I say, "My parents are really big on trust. They say it takes a long time to build it up, but a short time to lose it. You should trust Mr. Carpenter. He's a good guy. He's really smart too. He cares a lot about what he does."

I feel so weird saying this. I can feel Mr. Carpenter and Connelly looking at me like I just flew in from space on a UFO. But the statement serves me. She does need to trust him on the science, and it wouldn't hurt on the love front either. I've been taking inventory of other possible love interests for the President since we've been here, and I don't see anyone else who looks like they have enough nerve or enough youth to ask her out. All the dudes here are old or scurrying around like frightened mice. My best bet is to get her and Mr. Carpenter together. My plan is confirmed, as crazy as it may seem. I don't see any other way around it. Sorry, mom and dad. This project is still a go.

She nods in agreement and makes eye contact with Mr. Carpenter. He smiles and nods. I'm so glad he doesn't give her the thumbs up. That's very dorky, but also something he would totally do. "Well, ladies, it was so nice to meet you, but I have to get back to running the free world while it's still free." She laughs at her own joke and it seems like it is actually quite funny to her. She gets up and turns her back to us and walks toward her desk. When she does, I slip the last Post-it out of my pocket and slide it under a book on the table between the chair she sat in and my end of the couch. I leave a corner of the note sticking out so it can be seen. The little yellow square reads:

Naomi, There's no going back. Dinner? Call me. 555.3210. XO, Drew

I hop up quickly. I don't want to be sitting next to the note when she turns around. "Yes! I'm sure you have lots of decisions to make today," I say as I hurry towards the big white doors with golden handles that are as big as my arm. She waves goodbye as her phone rings. She answers it like TV President and we exit quickly.

"That was awesome, Daddy. Thank you. She's so beautiful and so much nicer than I imagined." Connelly seems genuinely delighted. I'm glad. Maybe it will take her mind off this morning and make our rushed shopping excursion worth it. As we leave the White House, I see how perfectly you can view the National Mall. I imagine it filled with climate crisis protestors. I imagine President Robinson standing there and looking out at a movement. I'm encouraged by today. I'm fired up. The thought of spending the rest of the day looking at frilly dresses makes me want to scream, especially when I could be working on my plans, but then I remember that homecoming is part of the plan. A sense of dread fills me. I do not want to go with Axl. I don't know him. I swallow back the dread and give Connelly my attention. She's prattling on about our dress shopping and directing Mr. Carpenter where to take us first. He's got to go back to the White House for a meeting but stays with us in Georgetown until he has to go. He is scared to leave us alone, but we convince him we will be okay. We agree to a lot of rules and finally he leaves us be.

The afternoon is pretty fun actually. We try on a million dresses that we can't afford. A smartly dressed gentleman too proper to ask us our age offers us champagne at one of the fancier stores and we gladly accept it. Sometimes it feels good to be bad. We end up at Rent the Runway and rent dresses for the dance. Mine is simple but nice. When you're tall and of average weight and don't really have hips or boobs (yet?), simple but nice works great, especially if you don't really care. The dress is the same color as one of the orange birds hanging in Dr. A's office. It's the kind of orange that's the inside of an orange not the outside of the orange, a little softer and more opaque. Sprinkled across the dress, there are seven, fierce tigers the size of quarters embroidered in golden thread. I love them. Each one is slightly different. If I have to wear a dress, a tiger dress is best.

Connelly chooses a dress the color of eggplant. It has all sorts of things going on. There's a ruffle at the bottom. One side is shorter. One strap is off the shoulder. I don't even know how it will stay on her. She seems happy though. Thankfully they have all the other things we need there too, and we don't have to go anywhere else. Connelly picks out accessories like shoes and jewelry. We try on no less than ten pairs of shoes each. I choose high heels that match the gold thread of my tigers. I walk around like I have eggs taped to the bottom of my feet. She gets a bejeweled headband for herself. I politely decline.

Mr. Connelly picks us up and we eat dinner at The Peacock Cafe before we head back to Longview. He tells that we made quite the impression on the President. I can't really imagine that's true, but it is nice of him to say. I ask him about their meeting and he says it went well. She listens, asks questions, takes notes. He admits she hasn't changed any of her policies or point of view, at least not yet. He says he's working on her. Earning and keeping her trust just like she described. I ask the universe to grow that trust into more. A big blooming consuming true love, thank you.

I fall asleep on the train back to Longview. The day included nearly every emotion I can think of. I close my eyes and risk a dream.

CHAPTER FOURTEEN

Thursday, September 19

I set my alarm for 5:01 AM. I only set my alarms to end in 1, 3 or 7. It's a thing. A superstitious thing. I have Queen Canary work to do before school. I go online and post the link to the classified report. With the report, I post the following:

> ➤ *Don't take it anymore. Stand up 4 yourself & Mother Earth. Meet @ ur school's flagpole 5 minutes before ur 1st bell. Stay 4 1 hour. Bring signs, fury, peace, hope.*

I post something to this effect on all my socials with the link and as many hashtags as I can come up with. I tag everyone I can think of that has influence including @thepresidentrobinson and @drewtheDCscienceguy. I tag Khalil and Khali's dad. My parents. My friends. My school. Khalil's school. Everyone I know checks their phone before school, so I know the message will get out. I do everything I can think of to make the posts go viral. I follow them up with additional posts that include pictures and quotes from the classified report. Ones that best summarize the conspiracy. I call out the schools that are the most targeted. I urge them to specifically to show up to the pole. I ask everyone to share the posts and tag their government officials and representatives. Then I turn my phone off. What's done is done. I get ready for school. I hug my mom and dad. They are waiting for me in the kitchen. My mom hands me a banana. I miss bacon. Then we go together to the flagpole.

I arrive at school an hour before it officially starts. I have no idea what if anything will happen. My mom and dad drag supplies from the Subaru and set up little stations around the flagpole. They bring poster boards, cardboard, sticks for handles, markers, waters, and granola bars. Moms gonna mom. I sit down in the grass near the flagpole. Phone still off. I just sit. I think. I breathe in for four and out for five. My parents sit beside me. We are quiet. I close my eyes for several minutes. Maybe I'm meditating? I'm not sure. I like it though. Maybe I fall asleep. I did get up early. When I open my eyes, tears spring out. As I look around, I see my classmates gathering. There are already 100 or more sitting, standing, or walking to the pole. They are wielding signs, flags and banners. Even our mascot, a 6.5 foot Lion is there with a gaggle of cheerleaders flanked by their athlete du jour. There are teachers, coaches, parents, and other staff too. No Principal Aguilera though. I can't believe it and I can believe it. What I've shared with the world is not okay. My classmates should be pissed. They should be here, and they are. By 7:25 AM, five minutes before the first bell, there are about 300 people gathered. My high school's population is 1,000. Not too shabby. We stay there for an hour and then silently move to our next class. It's peaceful and organized. The presence of the adults make it more legit somehow. If anyone was going to try to stop us, they didn't. I mentally take inventory of the adults that are there. Our allies. My parents don't make a big deal out of anything. They leave when the hour is up. That's part of our plan in an effort to remain anonymous. We suspect Principal Aguilera may give us some trouble once he figures it out.

I go to second block. I'm not nervous. I'm not anxious. I'm calm. I feel confident. I feel validated. Miss Starnes begins class without fanfare. She was at the flagpole too. She busies herself at the whiteboard, and I pull out my phone and turn it on. I look at my texts first. Hearts and the muscle arm emoji from my mom and dad. A question from Connelly asking if I'll be at the flagpole. I realize now that she wasn't there. A text from Khalil with a pic from the morning.

yo sis

mad people @ flagpole @ AS

dope

wut about LV

All Saints showed up. Longview showed up. Is it possible other schools showed up too? I can barely contain myself as I tap the little white bird icon on my phone. Apparently, it's possible, very freaking possible. The feed of @queencanary is flooded with retweets, pics, and posts. Schools from all over the East Coast showed up. Now schools from the Midwest are getting online, getting to school, and getting to their flagpoles. My eyes fill up again. Maybe I cry more than I thought I did. Or maybe life is just harder and more complex when you open your eyes and see what's going on around you?

As @queencanary I tap as many hearts as I can and retweet the pictures of small, medium, and large groups of students gathered at flagpoles. Miss Starnes catches me and I shove my phone into my bag before she confiscates it. I can't check it again until lunchtime. By noon, the school strike spreads across the U.S. Kids from coast to coast show up to fight for themselves and the environment. I am giddy, and now I'm nervous. What happens now? I can't wait to get home and go over the plan again with my parents. The response to the report is bigger than I thought, but it is just the beginning. I'm not naïve enough to think that one hour of kids striking school is going to upturn a world superpower's conspiracy. I grab my journal and write down a few ideas to talk through with my parents:

How to get to change

1. Strike longer

2. Strike more often
3. Strike with more kids
4. Get more adults involved
5. Get the media to the strikes
6. Say what we want to happen, what we want to change
7. Go bigger on the socials – everything viral, all the time
8. Ask for a response from the President and other officials
9. Make t-shirts, hats, signs, stuff and sell to raise money and awareness
10. Reveal my identity as @queencanary and go to Mr. Carpenter for help????

The last one makes me nervous. I'm not sure about it. Not sure if it will help or hurt. I certainly can't tell him before I tell Connelly. I need to talk to mom and dad about this one in detail. After seeing Mr. Carpenter with President Robinson, I am more and more convinced that he is a key ally and influencer to the world and especially to the President. If I tell him about @queencanary, my dream, the medium, and how I need his help, I think that could work. It could also completely flop. I don't want him to think that I'm crazy. I don't know what he knows about my dream about Mrs. Carpenter. I didn't think Khalil knew, but Connelly told him. Has Connelly told Mr. Carpenter? I don't know if he thinks precognitive dreams are possible or not. I don't know if he would be mad at me about Mrs. Carpenter or not. I guess it depends on if he believes in my gift. It's also risky because if he *does* think I'm a freak show, he might keep me from Connelly. I can't handle that.

That night, my parents and I lay out notebooks, pens, articles, calendars, books, and our laptops on the kitchen table. We scheme. We agree that the next step is critical. We go to bed exhausted and satisfied. It feels good to have them on my side. I know that I'm lucky like that.

CHAPTER FIFTEEN

Saturday, September 21

On Homecoming Day, I wake up to a complete and utter downpour. Partly, I'm grateful because it's a good excuse to stay in bed and work on my plans. Part of me worries that the heaving rain is a bad omen. I sing to myself, *like raaaaaaaaaaaiiiinnn on your Homecoming Day* in the style of The One and Only Alanis Morissette. I can't believe people my age don't know who she is. I spend the morning online. Posting, researching, retweeting, and finding pictures that tell the story. I also start a petition under the guise of @queencanary. I want to get as many signatures as I can to protest the school conspiracy and demand reform. I send it out into the Twittersphere. With it, I include the link to the classified report and ask for anyone interested in conducting a real investigation to contact @queencanary. This way, we can continue to add legit people to the fight. I need someone besides me carrying this torch. I'm hoping a newspaper like The Times or The Post will pick it up and help unveil the conspiracy. I get as much done as I can before noon. That's the time Connelly has directed me to be at her house ready for a full on Tiffany-esque make-over. I'm sweating just thinking about covering my face in a film of make-up. It's like a condom for your face. Although technically I've never touched one, but I can imagine the texture…I think. I should really look into that, especially if I am soon to take a lover.

I get to Connelly's and she's set up her room and her bathroom to look like an old-timey Hollywood dressing room. She's extra. It's kind of fun though. There are big bare bulbs on a string that she's hung around every mirror. I do feel a bit glamorous. She also has prosecco in water bottles for us. Not classy, but effective. I don't question where it came from. The less I know the better. She has all of our favorite songs from middle school on a playlist that is blaring. T Swizzle. Bruno Mars. Adele. The Biebs. Ed Sheeran. Drake. She throws in a little Dead just for me. She' not about that life. I love Connelly. She makes me laugh. She knows I am dreading this, and does her best to make it something that I'll enjoy. She has what looks to be torture devices lined up on her vanity. She assures me she will use them gently on my hair and they won't hurt a bit. I'm not convinced. There are pounds and piles of make-up stacked on every flat surface. She knows I can't pick, so she's set out a curated selection for me. What she'll do with the rest is beyond me. After a lot, a lot, a lot of manicuring and brushing and curling and tweezing and blending, she pronounces me ready for the ball.

I look at myself in the mirror. I do feel a little like Cinderella, *an orange dress with tigers on it wearing* Cinderella. I look a little longer and a little more closely. I barely recognize myself. It's not just the dress though or the make-up or the hair, it's me. I'm standing taller. I look confident. I look brave. I feel strong. Maybe it's the running or no more beef and lots more plants or the prosecco, but maybe it's that I feel purposeful. I feel like I'm making a difference. I'm proud of what I'm doing. I tilt my shoulders back a little more and lift my chin a little higher. I kick off the horribly, devastatingly uncomfortable shoes that are gorgeous, I'll give Connelly that, but they are meant to kill someone. Tonight's not about dying, it's about thriving. I slip my black and white checkered Vans back on. Now, I'm ready for the fucking dance.

Zach and Axl pick us up in Axl's mom's gas guzzling, jet-

black Tahoe and the four of us climb in. I think Mr. Carpenter
might pull Connelly back in the house at the last minute but he
doesn't. He just looks wistful and worried. As soon as we drive
off, the boys turn the music up way too loud. Travis Scott is
thumping through the speakers, the truck bumping in response.
We eat dinner at Katarina's. Everything is going pretty well. I
feel good. A whisper of a faint, happy buzz from the bottle of
prosecco that we split as we got ready hums through me. Confident. Secretly hopeful things will work out with Somewhat
Obnoxious Axl, so that I can just be done with my true love
mission. Throughout diner, Zack and Axl talk about the game
last night and the party they went to afterwards. I can tell this
is news to Connelly based on her surprised and hurt expression.
We did our regular FRYday night with her dad last night. She was
with me. I don't know where she thought Zach was. After our
dinner plates are cleared, I go to order dessert, but Axl redirects
me to "dessert" in the car.

In the car, there are Jell-O shots for days. How many could
one person consume? My question is quickly answered. Both
boys happily swish down four in a row. Thankfully, they have all
four before they realize that Connelly and I were just standing
there. They offer them to us. Pushing them in our direction.
Connelly selects two pink ones. One for each hand. I select a
red one from the middle of the plastic bowl. I bit it in half and
everyone laughs at me. I haven't been much of a drinker and certainly not drunk. My recent forays with champagne and prosecco are *not* all that I've ever had to drink but they represent
the volume. Two-ish glasses and that's it. I have to be careful
with my meds. My prosecco from this afternoon seems to have
disappeared under a huge salad piled with feta and flanked with
warm pita bread. I have to admit, I miss the faint fairy glow
of that baby-sized buzz. I bite the second half of my shot and
choose another one; this time orange like my dress.

By the time we get to school for the dance portion of the
evening, I am not drunk but I do feel lighter. Breezy. I hadn't

realized how much my dream, my plan, Mrs. Carpenter, untold truth to Connelly, the Guilt Dragon, and the heaviness of the climate crisis are weighing one me. It's heavy. It feels good to float just a tiny bit. Like a balloon that was given just enough helium to graze the ground. They boys on the other hand are full on flying. Their balloons are filled to the max, ready to pop.

The boys assure us that once we go in, we can't come back out. We need to finish strong. My defenses are lower this time; I grab another shot without hesitating. Connelly grabs two more pink ones and swallows them back fast. I can't keep count of the boys' shots. Maybe three or four more each? Since they are generally loud and obnoxious, they don't appear much different than normal to the chaperones who don't really know them anyways. They don't know them enough to tell that they are high-def versions of themselves as we stroll into the gym.

Connelly gasps with delight as we enter through the gym's steel doors. I'm looking down at my dress, checking for salad dressing or specks of Jell-O. I'm surprised to see nothing. That's impressive. Maybe I am growing up after all. Fuck you, Langdon. I look up to see what Connelly is fawning over. I suck my breath in too. The gym is transformed into a replica of Sub-Saharan Africa, home of the lions. Tall, thin, tan colored blades of grass are glued together to make a realistic image of the grasslands around the bottom half of all four walls of the gym. Strips of paper curl over and move like the grasslands when the students walk by. The horizon looks like a golden sunset. Crepe paper in every shade of orange, yellow, gold, indigo, purple and blue are layered on top of each other to create an ombre effect of light and color. There is a giant shadow of a black tree stationed in the middle of each wall. Crepe paper twisted together to give the tree dimension. The top branches coming up over the top of the wall and climbing to meet in the center of the gym's ceiling. The lights are off and there are hundreds of fairy lights giving the room the glow of a starry dusk. It's very *Lion King* meets *Enchanted.* It's romantic. I can't believe I'm even thinking that.

Maybe it is the magic of the gym's transformation or the Jell-O shots talking, but I tap into my inner Nala and grab Axl's hand to pull him on the dance floor. He comes easily. The music is its own heartbeat. I can feel it in my body, massaging my bones as I dance. Now I know for sure that it's at least a little bit of the alcohol talking because I dance without worry of being talked about or laughed at. I just dance. I give a silent thanks to my mom for making me go to jazz and hip-hop classes back in elementary school. I at least have a vague sense of the music and how to make my body work. Axl is into it. He's hopping around and throwing his arms up. He looks happy. I feel happy.

After a few songs, we take a break. I'm starting to sweat and I don't think Connelly will approve of my make-up sliding off my face. We make our way to the refreshments. They are kind of cute. Animal crackers, the plain kind (gross) and the kind with the pink and white frosting with the dot shaped sprinkles (delicious). I grab a handful. I will have dessert after all, suckers. They have other stuff that is lion inspired, like a big lion's face and mane made out of orange carrots, yellow peppers, and light brown crackers. All the crackers are arranged in a big circle to represent a lion's head. There were two olives for the lion's eyes, but someone ate one and now he's a winking or sleepy lion. There are orange cupcakes with little lion faces artfully made with think black icing. I take one of those too. There's a sign that says "The Watering Hole" above the drinks. We finish our snacks and head back to the dance floor.

The final notes of a fast-paced song end and the soft notes of a slow song fill the gym. It's a relief. I'm getting tired. Axl pulls me close to him. It feels nice to be held. I've been holding a lot. I don't hate dancing with Axl. I thought it would be worse. There's nothing that special about him to me. I haven't gotten the impression that we have much in common. If it weren't for the music and the dancing, I'm not sure what we would do or talk about. But in this moment, under the fairy lights and with the music swallowing the room. It's good enough. It's kind of nice. We dance to a few more songs. Then Axl wants to make the rounds before we get ready to go. I don't really know what that means, so I make my way back to the refreshments. I notice Connelly and Zach in the corner of the gym. Connelly looks upset. Zach looks angry. I watch them for a few minutes. Then I start making my way to them. Connelly looks like she is getting more upset.

I go to them. I reach for Connelly's hand. "What's going on? What's wrong?"

"He wants to drive us home, but I don't think he should. I don't think he or Zach should drive. What do you think?" She's whimpering a little. I hadn't thought about that at all. I have no idea how much is too much or how long you should wait before driving. Is it like swimming? Like 30 minutes after you eat? If so, they are probably fine. I really don't know. I have no experience. I look at Zach. He seems okay. Not bad. Not like wild or throwing up or anything like that. In fact, he looks like of subdued. He is acting better than normal. I side with Zach. I tell them I think everything will be fine if one of the boys drives us back. It isn't that far.

Connelly looks at me like I slapped her. I know instantly that I've made some sort of mistake. Girl code violation. Zach takes this as his cue and goes to find Axl. He says to meet them at the car in five minutes.

"Gosh dangit. You *are* crazy, Simone. You're as crazy now as you have ever been. Feeling overwhelmed and depressed again? So much so that you want to die again? Want to get in the car with drunk boys and get killed? Is that what you want? Is that what you always want? Is it the attention? Is it the notoriety? Is that the only way you think you'll ever be popular, SAM? To be the craziest one of us all?" She's loud but not louder than the music.

I can't believe she's saying this to me. She's never said anything this harsh to me ever. Never. I can't take it. I feel like

I'm going to burst. Blood swishes in my temples. My eyes fill with tears. My heart is breaking. Maybe she's finally had it with me. Finally had it with all my drama and dreams and high-maintenance needs. Maybe she can't take anymore of me stealing the spotlight with all my issues while she's trying to grieve the death of her mom, one of the best in the world. Her volcano is erupting, and it's because of me. I can't take this. I can't do it. I can't hear any more of this. I am so angry. So embarrassed. So hurt. The Guilt Dragon stirs from its slumber and stretches out in my body. He's takes up all the space in a matter of moments. I do the only thing I know to do. I run.

I run past my classmates. Curious heads turn to see me, yes me, crazy ol' me, running for the heavy gym doors. I push the metal handle and am deposited into the darkness of the late night sky. I'm starting to hyperventilate, so I stop running. I'm about a block away from the school. I put my hands on my knees. I bend over and gasp for breath. Gasp for answers. What just happened? I stay like this for a few moments until I can get my breath under control. I stand up and feel someone next to me. I hadn't heard anyone come up. My crying and breathing were too loud to hear over. It's Axl. I sigh with relief.

"Hey," he says. "What's wrong? What happened? We were having a great time. I was saying bye to everyone, and then suddenly I see you sprinting for the door." He reaches for my hands and pulls me to him. He strokes what's left of my hair. I'm spent. I let him. He touches my cheek and wipes away the tears and streaks of black mascara. "It's okay," he says. "I'm here. I got you." I am feeling calmer. It's nice to be hugged. Feeling held is something I didn't know I was missing in my life. I lay my head on his shoulder. My sobs turn to softer cries. Axl rubs my back. It feels nice. He pulls me even closer to him. I can feel his legs against mine, his hips in line with mine. He kisses the space between my neck and my shoulder. I'm surprised, but not upset. I'm curious more than anything. My tears slow. I'm distracted from the fight with Connelly. My attention now on Axl and what he's doing to me. He pulls the strap of my dress down so that it lines up at the bottom of my shoulder. He runs his fingers from my jaw, down my neck, and across my shoulder until gets to the strap. Then he pulls the strap down so that my small, breast is exposed. I'm excited looking at my own body in the moonlight. Axl rubs his thumb along the edge of me. He takes his time. He repeats the circular motion. He pulls my whole body into his. I think I can feel him hardening between my legs, but I'm not sure. How can you tell? How do I know what is what? I don't know how I feel about this.

He asks me, "Do you like this?"

"Yeah, umm, I think so. Yeah." I'm blushing. I've never felt anything like this before in my life. Ten minutes ago my best friend was breaking my heart and now Axl is putting my body back together. He takes my hand and leads me off the sidewalk and to a side road behind a line of cars. He picks up where he left off. He moves to my mouth and kisses me. It's not gentle, it's almost rough. Suddenly, I can't breathe. This is all happening too fast. I'm not sure I want any of this anymore. I push off his shoulders. "I need some air." I try to say this with a laugh in my voice. Light. Be light again.

"No, you don't." He's not laughing. He grabs my hand and places it between his legs. I jerk my hand back. "What's wrong? You were into it like one minute ago." His voice is full of accusation. "I was. I mean I am. I think. I just need a minute. I don't know what I'm doing. I don't know what's happening."

"Ah, I've heard this about you Simone. A lot bit crazy, and a little bit of a tease, but worth it since you're a virgin, I'm assuming." He reaches for my hand again. "NO, AXL." My voice is high and loud. A tinge of panic in it. He grabs both wrists and pushes me against one of the nearby cars. As he does, the car alarm goes off. "What the fuck?" he demands angrily. He takes one look at me and says, "Nah, not worth it. They were wrong. Too much crazy for me. I'm out."

He leaves me there and jogs nonchalantly back towards the school. I panic. The alarm is still going off, and I'm still up against the passenger side door. I need to get out of here. The only thing I want to do is crumple into a little ball even if it is on the side of the road. I pull myself together. I don't have a choice. I take a deep breath. I look back up at Axl as he runs away. As I watch him, I see smoke in the distance. Coming from the school. Near the gym. The boiler room. Damnit.

I reach for my phone. I need to call 911. I don't have my phone on me because I'm wearing a dumb dress with no pockets. My phone is in my little purse that Connelly made me get. All that stuff is in the gym. I forgot it in my panicked hurry to get the hell out of there. Shit. Shit. Shit. I scream into the night. Why? Why does so much bad stuff have to keep happening? Why am I the one that has to deal with everything? Why can't anything just be fun and simple and safe? I take one more moment to lament thoughtless, greedy Axl, then I fill my lungs with air and I run back to the school as fast as I can.

When I get to the gym, I try to get back inside but the chaperones won't let me in. I try to tell them what I see. The smoke. Back behind the gym. The students are in danger. Everyone needs to get out. Now. I tell them I need to find my friend. Connelly. She has blonde hair. Purple dress. I babble on about my dream. The school. The fire. Just another example of the conspiracy. I'm loud and a little out of control. I can feel myself slipping. I cry loudly. Snot runs down my face like my nose is a faucet. A group of adults and kids gather around me. They try to calm me down, but aren't successful. I'm screaming for someone to call 911, but a teacher keeps telling me there's no smoke. They sent someone to check. There's no smoke? I don't understand what's happening. I look up again and search from what I'd seen in the sky near the car. There's nothing there.

I hear kids talking. Whispering. Jeering. I hear the words "witch" and "crazy" and "psychic" and "psycho." I hear laughter. Not gentle, happy laughter, but mean mocking laughter. I swear

I hear Langdon and Axl burning me at the stake. Where is Connelly? What am I supposed to do now? I panic. I can't think. I need more air. I need space. I'm burning with embarrassment and shame. I stare down at my tiger dress and realize how stupid they are, how insane I am. I need to get out of here.

My house isn't far. A ½ mile or so from school. I know the way inside and out. Tonight it seems longer. Darker and scarier. Every noise makes me jump and scream. I'll be home in less than ten minutes. The irony of the beginning of this night's demise isn't lost on me. We didn't even need a ride home. We could have just walked to my house. It's a little further but we could have even walked back to Connelly's. Maybe she was thinking that the whole time. It would have been harder for her in her lilac stilettos but not impossible. My parents aren't expecting me. The plan was to stay at Connelly's after the dance. I can't sneak in. Cherry Garcia will give me away even if my parents don't see me. I can't keep walking to Connelly's. It's clear she doesn't want me there. I think of excuses to tell my parents. They won't believe that Connelly went somewhere with the boys after the dance. Mr. Carpenter wouldn't allow that. I decide on the truth or at least part of the truth. I'll tell them Connelly and I have a fight. We have about one a year so this will be it.

I'll leave the rest of the night out. No talk of stupid Axl and what he did to me. No talk of the nonexistent fire and my freak out over nothing. No mention of my classmates mocking me and calling me all the names I fear are true about myself. I won't tell them the kids I've known for years and how they exposed my every insecurity and called them out self-importantly for everyone to hear. I won't tell them how wonderful the night started out. How confident I felt. How lightly I floated. I won't tell them how that high turned into a low. I won't tell them the shame I feel. I won't say anything about the doubt I feel about myself. I'll keep all that inside, hidden away.

I'll stick to the Connelly story. We have *never* had a fight like this. She's never talked to me like that. She's never talked to anyone like that. Is that how she really feels about me? Is that what she's wanted to say to me for the past year? I don't blame her. I'm just shocked she actually said those words aloud, to my face, at school. My heart breaks again at the thought of her hissing at me. Her face was tight with anger and disappointment. Her petite hands clenched at her sides. Her body pulling away from mine.

I stand at the front door. I catch my breath. I smooth my dress. I wipe off my backside as best I can. I don't have my purse. No mints or a hairbrush or even that damn cherry lip-gloss. I can't really tidy up, and I'm certain I look like an abandoned, broken-legged, flea-infested kitten. Fuck. I turn the knob and by the grace of the universe, the door swings open. I catch it before it does its traditional bang against the hallway wall. Cherry Garcia is at my feet instantly. Not barking. He doesn't really bark, but lets out clogged snorts. I scoop him up and bury my mascara stained face into the side of his warm body. My parents aren't downstairs but they hear me come in. My mom hollers down from the bonus room.

"Hello? Is someone down there? Simone Alice Marker, is that you?"

"Yeah, mom. It's me. I'm home."

"What's wrong? Are you okay? Where's Connelly?" She sounds worried. Of course. Why wouldn't she be? My mom. She should have been in the FBI.

"Mom, everything is fine. I'm just really tired. Been a big couple of weeks you know. I decided to come home after the dance."

"Of course, you are, honey. Of course. Also, I'm sure the social aspect of tonight was a lot for you."

Thanks, mom for remembering that I'm socially awkward. She's coming downstairs now. Nothing is keeping her from seeing her baby. She talks as she walks. I keep the lights off and hope she does too. No need to shine a light onto my tear-stained, puffy, wild-eyed face.

"You looked gorgeous in the pictures you sent! Did you have fun? What was it like?"

"Thanks, mom. Yeah, it was fun. The gym looked cool. Like the desert, like where a lion lives."

I'm in the powder room now trying to fix my face. She would not think I look gorgeous right now. She's downstairs now.

"Simone, where are you? What are you doing?" She continues her line of questioning. FBI. "In the powder room, Mom. Just washing my face off. You know I can't stand all that make-up Connelly put on me. Trying to get it off before it causes even more pimples."

"You only ever have one pimple at a time, dear." Thanks for noticing, Agent Mom. She's waiting for me when I come out of the bathroom. Hands on hips. Cherry Garcia standing guard at her feet. Mad I didn't let him into the bathroom with me. She looks me over. I'm doing my best to radiate normalcy. I'm normal. Normal. Normal. I rearrange my face in a couple of different ways trying to get it to lay flat. Normal. "Everything, okay?" Mom asks gently.

"Yep. I'm great. Just tired. And hungry. You know how I get when I'm hungry. I'm going to grab a snack and hit the hay." Hit the hay? What am I? 80 years old? My forced cheerfulness is aging me. Be more normal than that, Simone. Geez. "Alright. Well, come here and give me a good-night hug." She pulls me in to her. This hug is the hug I really needed tonight. I bite my bottom lip to keep from crying. I let my mom hold on to me longer than I typically do. She pats my back. Then extends her arms and looks at me closely.

"If you ever need to talk about anything, you know that I'm here for you. No matter what. I hope the last few weeks has reminded you of that. You are not alone. You never have to go through anything alone. Anything." I nod. I do know. Maybe tomorrow I'll want to tell her everything about tonight. The good and the bad. The beautiful and the ugly. But right now. I want nothing more than to sleep. I don't even think about the possibility of having another Big One like I do every other night. I just want to close my eyes and feel nothing else tonight. My mom lets go of me and walks into the kitchen. I just stand there in the hallway. She brings back a granola bar and a tall glass of water. "See you in the morning, Simone Alice Marker. I love you."

"Love you, Mom" I croak. I want her to tell Dad that I said good night and I love him, but I can't get all that out. I take the stairs by twos. It feels like an Olympic feat. My body is exhausted. I flop down on my bed and bury my head in my pillow. I let out a few screams deep into the down. I fall asleep almost instantly. I've never been happier to escape.

CHAPTER SIXTEEN

Sunday, September 22

My parents let me sleep until noon and then they check on me. I know my mom is worried, so I force myself to seem cheerful. I suggest we go to lunch. I'm starving and it seems like a good distraction. I miss my phone as if I lost a limb. Did Connelly text me last night? Did Axl? Has anyone reached out to me about investigating the classified report? I haven't posted anything on behalf of Queen Canary in almost 24 hours. Has anyone important responded to some of my more scathing Tweets? President Robinson? Mr. Carpenter? How is my petition doing? Shoot, I'd even be up for one of Khalil's new songs. That's a social Cardinal sin. I need my phone back from the gym ASAP. Our lunch outing is a good distraction. We decide to ride our bikes ten miles to the next town over. There is a new vegan restaurant, The Lima Bean, that we want to try. We are running out of plant-based ideas at home. We need some inspiration.

At lunch we talk next steps. I don't think we can wait around for others to respond to us. I have to keep taking action. The more I do, the more likely the influencers will respond or do something to help. We plan another school strike for Thursday. Maybe it becomes a weekly thing? I think this one needs more of a call to action. We brainstorm what it could be. I have the petition online. I think I can tie it to that. Meet at the flagpole. Stay an hour. Sign the petition. Make sure everyone at your flagpole does too. It's something.

When I get home, I get out my journal. I need to process last night. Dr. A would agree. I write and write and write. I write about my overdose last year. I write about Axl. What felt good and how surprising that was, what felt terrible and how terrifying that was. Tears splash the page when I recount him grabbing my hands and putting them on his body. I cry more when I remember how scared I was when he pushed me against that car. What was he going to do? I'm so angry at him. Anger is better than depressed for me though. I can action anger. Depression smothers me into a silent suffering statue. I write about my gratitude for the car alarm and for wearing my Vans and for my mom. It feels good to get out of my body and mind and onto the paper. Get it out.

I reach for my phone to text Connelly, and remember I that I still don't have it. I want to tell her everything. I want to tell her how sorry I am for not being there for her like she needed me to. I want her to know that I know that she's the strong one but she shouldn't have to be. I should've been able to be her rock and not the other way around. I want to ask for her forgiveness. I want to tell her about my dream again. I want to tell her about her mom's message. I want to ask her if she wants to be a part of the plan now that we know more about why her mom got sick. I want her to know that everything I'm doing, I'm doing for her, for Mr. Carpenter, for Mrs. Carpenter, for all of us. I want to tell her the truth about the dates and why I need them, why I need to find true love. I want to know what she thinks about her mom's message. I want her to know her mom believes in love, for whatever that's worth. For whatever that might mean to Connelly. I'll have to wait. Monday is only one sleep away. What's the worst that could happen?

CHAPTER SEVENTEEN

Monday, September 23

I'm anxious to get to school and find my phone. I race through breakfast, take my meds, and don't even bother with my layers. I manage a decent ponytail. No major zits to deal with today. Miracles on miracles. A baby-t with the mushroom from Super Mario is my shirt of the day. I found it at Goodwill. Jeans. My pink Vans. Go. I wait impatiently for Cherry Garcia to do what he needs to do. Then, I'm off.

At school, I rush to the office while begging the universe to let my purse be in the lost and found. I wait in a line of other disgruntled and needy students for my turn with the school secretary. She's annoyed by the time she gets to me. I don't blame her. I explain what happened. I forgot my purse at the dance. I'm hopeful someone turned it in. Maybe a chaperone? I describe what it looks like. Brown faux suede with fringe. Small. Moon shaped. The secretary tells me to wait at the desk and she goes to see what if anything was turned in. A teacher stops her on her way and they talk about the weekend and the weather. OMG. Come on. I need my phone. If it's not there, I am not sure where to look. Maybe Connelly picked it up for me? Will she give it back? Will she even talk to me? My hands slick with sweat at the thought of telling her everything I need to tell her. Besides all the dream stuff, and my plans, I also need a friend. I need to tell her about Axl. I want her to tell me that I didn't do anything wrong. That Axl's a jerk. That it's normal that I didn't want to touch him like that, especially given the situation.

I wait patiently for a few more minutes and then call out to the secretary in the nicest voice I can muster, "Excuse me. M'am, did you find my purse? I need to get going to class." She stops talking, rolls her eyes, tells the other teacher bye, and then continues her search for my purse. She rounds the corner triumphantly, like she did something really great. I am so happy though that I clap for her. She hands it to me and I eyeball the contents. The only thing that matters is there. I sigh with relief. It's dead and I have no charger or place to charge it. My school isn't down with people plugging in around campus. I pull it out to examine it. Honestly I want to hug it. There's a big scratch down the front. Dangit. I wonder how that happened. I don't remember dropping it although maybe I did. Or maybe someone else did? Who was looking at my phone?

If I hurry, I can make it to my locker before first block. I hope Connelly is there. No muffin required. I just want to see her face. When I round the corner, there's no Connelly. There's no one. But there is a piece of paper, a note, taped to my locker. I snatch it off the blue and gold locker and read it. It's on school letter head. A lion watermark in the middle of the paper.

Come see me in my office. ASAP.

Principal Aguilera

I crumple the letter and stuff it in my pocket. What is this about? The dance? The drinking? Axl? The fight with Connelly? My grades? Queen Canary? I hate the feeling that I'm in trouble. Hate it. My heart beats faster. I wring my cool, sweaty hands. It's time to go to first block. I'm choosing class over the office.

That's a good excuse at least. In first block, I think about when I'm going to see Connelly next. Our schedules are so different this year. I'm going to go to our usual table at lunch. With or without her. Maybe she will meet me there. I can't text her to see.

At lunch I make my way to our table. She's there. With Zach. There's no room for me. My face is hot. It's a slap in the face. What is going on with her? This is not her. Not my Connelly. I turn quickly on my heel and bolt back the way I came. Tears threaten to spill out. I beeline for the upper soccer field. No one is ever there. Even though I feel lonely, I also want to be alone. That's a dangerous combo when your brain works like mine. I know I need to do something productive or I'll start to spin. I sit down under the bleachers and pull my journal from my backpack. I write.

Dear Connelly,

You are my dearest and best friend. I love you with all my heart. You are more like a sister than a friend. I'm worried that what I've been keeping from you is keeping us apart. This letter is a confession. Bear with me. I need to get this off my chest.

Since I had my latest Big One, I've been doing things behind your back. I am so ashamed. Not of what I've done, but that I've done it without you. It started at the Sixth Sense Conference.

Connelly-your mom came through to me from the medium. I can't believe it's taken me this long to tell you. I'm so sorry. I didn't know how. I didn't know if you'd believe me. She gave me a message. I've been using that message to create plans to save the planet from the climate crisis. I know that sounds nuts. It does to me too, but I know in my heart that it's true. I know I have the mission and the guts to do this. I have the motivation. Your mom is my motivation. My relationship with you is my motivation. I would do anything for you.

Her message was this...I think you need to hear it too. Your mom told me to forgive myself. I'm trying really hard to do that for her and for me. You know it isn't easy for me, but now I at least owe her that. I hope you'll forgive me too. I know you say you have, but I guess I can't accept your forgiveness until I forgive myself.

She also told me that the true love is the answer. Does that mean anything specific to you, Connelly? I'm trying to figure out what that means given what I'm trying to do with climate change and everything. It doesn't make sense to me yet. I don't really know what she meant, so I've been doing everything I can think of to find true love. That's why I've been dating. I tricked you into helping me by letting you take the blame for some of the distance between us. It's not your fault. It's mine. I've been keeping secrets from you.

Since I don't exactly know what she meant, I've been thinking of other people that would need to find true love too in order to make climate change better. I know the President needs to change her mind about climate change. That's the fastest way out of this climate mess. So, -- brace yourself--I'm trying to get the President to find true love too.

You might never forgive me for this, but I'm so desperate that I've even been thinking of ways to get your dad to find true love. This is the part that you might hate me for—but, maybe even with the President. Like your dad and the President as a couple. She needs someone she loves enough and trusts enough to change her mind. I thought maybe your dad could be that guy. This sounds so crazy. I know. I can't believe I'm putting this in writing.

I wonder if your mom wanted you to find true love too. Maybe you have that in Zach? That's what I'm hoping because I want you to have true love. I want you to be happy. I think that's what your mom wants for all of us. <u>I'm starting to think that is all that everyone needs</u>. Enough love in each of us to want to be different, to do different, to make sacrifices, to take a stand. To love someone or something so much that you'll fight for it. You'll fight for a place to love that person. To love your dog or your cat or your fish. To love water and air and beach and sun. To love so hard and so much that you won't stop until you it's safe and secure. To love so deeply that you'll do anything: make yourself a laughing stock, be the weird, crazy, psychic kid—or even lie to your best friend.

I'm so sorry I've been keeping this from you. I feel awful. I'm sick about it. I've been meaning to tell you, and I can never get the words out right. They are coming out all wrong now too, but at least you'll know the truth.

There's more.

I'm also Queen Canary. I'm the person behind the viral climate crisis stuff. Those are all my accounts. I have to fulfill my mission, Connelly. I can't let what happened to your mom happen again. I hope you don't hate me because I love you. I need you.

I look up from my scribbles and check the time on my phone. I only have a few more minutes. I need to finish this.

Connelly-Be mad at me. Hate me a little if you need to, but then please forgive me. Please join me. Please let's just be us again. I have so much to tell you. Something bad happened to me after I left the dance. I haven't told anyone. It has to do with Axl. He did something bad to me. I need to talk. Please call me.

Simone + Connelly. SAM + CONN. Love.

I sign it and fold it in half. I jog back to her locker and drop it through the slot as fast as I can.

At home that afternoon, I finally get my phone working again. It takes me hours to go through the texts and tweets and updates on my socials. I am overwhelmed by it all, but in a good way. It's a nice distraction from my day and the letter I left in Connelly's locker. I check on my petition. It has over 100,000 signatures on it. I dance around my room. Just a few more sleeps before we gather for *Flock This Thursdays*. It's what the Flock named our now weekly protests.

I post more content about the climate crisis. Lots of pictures of animals and homes and food destroyed by climate change. Part of me wonders if I should try another tactic. I think about the letter that I wrote Connelly and everything I wrote about love. Maybe there is something about love and loving our planet that should be part of my campaigns. I post a picture of Cherry Garcia and caption it: *Do it for love. Do it for all of us. Do it now.* #whydoyoufight #whodoyoulove #flockthisthursday #climatecrisis #reform #schoolconspiracy #takeaction #findtruelove #savetheplanet #doitforthelove

People love dogs. Within seconds, The Flock is posting pictures of the things, people, animals, and places they love. They use the same set of hashtags and add even more. Everyone's pictures look so happy and full of life. So different than the ones I've been posting of starving animals and desolate landscapes. Maybe people need to remember the good stuff they love. Maybe that is the motivation. *Why else would all this matter?* What would we be saving the planet for if it weren't to protect everything we love? I add another Tweet.

> ➤ *@ the pole this week, bring a picture of what u luv. Show them why it matters.*

Bold with the good vibes, I text my dad and ask him how we to plan a protest in D.C.. He texts back to come downstairs like a normal human and we can talk about it. I do. We do some research and my dad fills out online paperwork to secure us a date. He tells me he'll let me know when he hears back. I go upstairs to finish catching up. I need more media attention. The Flock is doing great, but we need a *story* not just posts and pictures. We need airtime. We need to go bigger.

I research journalists. I find one who covered a bunch of kids down in Georgia who put together a movement to protest gun violence in their community. I read all the articles that the journalist wrote about the students. They are amazing. They organized themselves so quickly and planned big events just like the one I have in mind. They did it all on their own. Essentially no adult supervision. They even hold press conferences all over the country aimed at educating people about gun control and gun violence prevention. They run think tanks on the topic too. *I can do all this.* I just need more help. I send the journalist a summary of what I've done and what I want to do. I send him a link to the classified report. I ask him to help us. I send a little prayer into the universe. Let this work.

More help. I need more help. I wonder if I need to reveal my identity. A few people might recognize me from my Cherry Garcia post, but not many. Thankfully he looks like every other pug that ever existed. I still haven't dealt with Principal Aguilera either. I don't know what he knows or why he wants to talk to me. I've been avoiding the office, but I can't for much longer. I want Connelly's help and Mr. Carpenter's for sure. I need to talk to Connelly.

I check my phone again to see if she's called or texted, but nothing. Nothing over the weekend when I didn't have my phone and nothing today. The little dig in my heart is enough to warrant going to bed. I'm exhausted. It's a lot of emotional responsibility to carry this torch, plus deal with all the other stuff in my life like Connelly and Axl and pre-cal. I shudder at the memory of Saturday night. I feel sick for two reasons.

1. I can't believe he did that to me, and I don't know what to do about it. I need Dr. A's help processing everything. This Friday will be a big session. Actually they are all big sessions these days. She's probably tired too.
2. I'm back to square one with my own quest for love, and right now I don't even have Connelly to help me. I pick up my phone and go to Yubo. I do some scrolling

and swiping. Gross. I hate this so much. Every guy I see makes me feel nauseous. I don't know anything about these people. What if they do something like Axl did to me? Or Worse? I fall asleep thinking about non-Yubo ways to find true love.

CHAPTER EIGHTEEN

Tuesday, September 24

I haven't heard anything from Connelly about the letter I slipped into her locker. Typically fighting with Connelly would be the only thing I think about, but I have so much on my mind that I'm not thing about it non-stop When I do think about it, I am sick to my stomach. Why hasn't she responded to my letter? Not even a text. I haven't seen her all week. I mean I've seen her. She's at school, but she's not coming near me. It's breaking my heart. I am realizing how alone I am at school. If she is abandoning me, I really need to make some new friends. God, I hope she's not. Please let this be a tiny bump in the road. I'm so lonely.

After school, I'm antsy. I can feel myself fighting all the feelings I don't want to feel. Thank goodness I'm really excited about Thursday's protest. It's keeping me afloat. There's a lot of energy and excitement around the planned protest. I guess that's what happens when you give people more than a few hours notice. @queencanary is going strong. More and more followers by the hour, it seems. Now we just need to turn that momentum into action and change. It's all so overwhelming though. Between feeling borderline depressed about Connelly and overwhelmed about saving the planet, I'm in a sensitive place. I need to monitor my mind. I could easily slip into a dark place with all that's going on. I consider my tools. Write. Breathe. Talk. Meditate. Run. I settle on a run. It will give me an excuse to go by Khalil's house. That could also be a talk. Two tools is better than one.

I've been thinking about him a lot lately. More than is normal for a friend like Khalil. He's been so helpful with Queen Canary and so supportive of me. He makes me feel like I don't have to prove myself. I can be myself around him. I'm beginning to think that maybe I *should* give him a chance. Now that he's not texting me every day, I kind of miss his songs and his flirting. Geez, when I compare the fact that he's a little annoying to the others I've been on dates with recently, he looks like winner of "The Bachelorette" material. A talk with Khalil will be nice. It will help. If nothing else, a friendly face. Someone that I know wants to hang out with me.

I change into a sports bra, white tank top, and green 70's looking running shorts. The kind with white piping around the edges. I grab my Asics. They have a vintage vibe that I like. I braid my hair into two shorter braids on the sides of my head. I look at myself in my bathroom mirror. Wait, am I trying to look cute? For a run? To see Kahlil? I think I am. Oh, shit. I'm even considering lip-gloss. I skip it. That's weird. I do dab a little vanilla oil on my wrists. I don't know what I'm doing. I just need to go.

My heart races even before I start running. What is happening? Am I? No. Am I? Really? Do I? Is Khalil my true love? No way. No. Not after all this time. Why is life so complicated?

Before I get to Khalil's, I stop and dab the sweat from my face with my forearm. I sniff at my armpits. Thank goodness for the drops of vanilla. I pat my braids down a little bit. I walk slowly to catch my breath. Why didn't I get dressed and just walk over here a like normal person? Maybe because that would have made this moment too real. Too much of what I'm now hoping it will be. The more I thought about it on the way here, the more sense it makes. He's my friend. He loves me already. He knows ALL my secrets, and that's a lot. He loves me anyways or maybe even because of them. He's known me forever. The smile on my face is gigantic. I can't believe it took me this long to get it. To get how amazing he is. To get how good we could be together.

I take a deep breath and nervously ring the doorbell. I wait for what seems like forever. Someone answers the door. It's not Khalil. Or Mr. Williams. Or Mrs. Rivers-Williams. Or Khalil's little brother, Khori. It's a girl. A gorgeous girl. A gorgeous girl who is my age. She vaguely familiar but I don't know why. We are staring at each other. She has a lovely, calm, welcoming expression. I can't imagine what mine looks like. Confused, I guess. Who is this? Connelly is his only girl cousin. A babysitter for Khori? A long lost relative. Please let her be someone he's related to. Please. Please.

"Hi. You're Simone!" She reaches through the door to hug me. Hug me. Who is hugging me? Where is Khalil? "I've heard so much about you. I've been reading all your Queen Canary stuff." She puts a finger to her lips to indicate a secret. A secret I had with Khalil. Not this girl. Whoever she is. "Come in! I'm so glad you're here. Come in. Come in." Who does she think she is inviting *me* into the Williams' house? Why is she being so nice? I still haven't said a word, but I let her lead me inside. A house that I've been in a million times. Seriously though, where is Khalil?

"I'm Moriah." She reaches for my hand like we're grown-ups at a business meeting. She nods her head gently at me as if that will help me snap out of it and agree to do what she's doing.

"Oh," I say. "Hi, I'm Simone Marker," I stammer. She laughs.

"I know, silly! I just said that."

"Oh," I say again. "Where is Khalil? I'm here to see Khalil." She laughs a little as she says this but her effervescence seems to simmer one little notch. She responds kindly, "Yeah,

I figured. He's upstairs with Khori. They are in the middle of a heated video game. Something with sports." She shrugs. This I can agree with. I don't get it either. "Let's go see if we can convince them to end it already. Come on."

She takes my hand again. Who is this? Why does she look familiar? Before I can take a step or ask a question, Khalil bounds down the stairs whooping with victory. Khori is standing at the top of the stairs pouting and throwing Legos at us. In his victory triggered testosterone induced mania, Khalil rushes to Moriah and lifts her high off the ground. So much time at the gym. She squeals with delight. I didn't know people could really make that sound. She whispers something in his ear. He turns his head and finally sees me still standing like an abandoned statue in the doorway. Puzzle pieces start to fall into place. Fewer texts. Fewer songs. Us. We. Mysterious absences. He takes two big steps towards me and tugs on a braid.

"Hey stranger. Sup, kid." Sup, kid? Sup, kid? Be normal. Breathe. Breathe some more. "This is Moriah. Remember, I told you about her and her twin sister? From my school?" I nod my head slowly. But why do I know her?

"You'll never guess what happened." H e doesn't wait for me to guess. "She went to that psychic guy that you went to. The conference thing. I didn't see her when I was watching the Livestream. Must have been when it was buffering, which was lot. But she was there. She got a message or whatever ya call it. You'll never guess what hers was." Expectantly, he looks at me to make a guess. "I don't know." I manage to spit out. One shoulder half shrugs. I want to lay down and sleep for the winter like a bear. I can feel my insides get a little darker as we stand here awkwardly.

"Her message was to give ME a chance!" He throws his head back in laughter. He is so happy. "And she did! Simone, I got a girlfriend! I finally got a girlfriend, and I got a HOT girlfriend." He looks to Moriah in response to her *tsktsk*. "I mean beautiful. I respectfully think that she is beautiful. On the outside. AND the inside. She's very smart and funny and kind." He finishes the last part fast so she can't *tsktsk* him again. He glows.

I missed my chance. It took me too long to see it. He's moved on and apparently to someone amazing. I know I need to say something. Be normal. "That's really great, Khalil. It's about time." I attempt a joke. It's half-hearted.

"That's what's up." He tries to fist bump me but my arms are limp at my sides. I want to sleep. "Yo, are you alright? You're acting weird. Weirder than normal." He jokes back. I swallow the thickness in my throat. "Yeah, I'm fine. I just ran over here. It's still so hot out. I'm a little lightheaded I think I just need to go home. Get some water. Something to eat maybe"

"On it!" Moriah jumps at the chance to help me. She does seem really nice. "'I'll get us all some snacks." I'm hurt and angry but Khalil has no idea know why. In his mind, I've been rejecting him since middle school. Why should I care about Moriah now? I lash out at him anyways. "Why did you tell her about Queen Canary?" I hiss fiercely. "That was *our* secret." There are sharp, salty tears desperately trying to escape from behind my eyes. Get back in there, I will them.

"Woah, chill. I don't know. I was helping you out. Posting all that stuff. Liking everything. She noticed. We got to talking about it. She's really into that stuff too. Like the climate stuff *and* the fortune telling stuff." As if I don't know what stuff he's talking about. No wonder Khalil was all about the climate crisis. He fooled Mr. Williams and me. "Y'all have a lot in comm..." I cut him off without hesitation. Embarrassment and a bout of heartache bubble inside me.

"Thanks a lot, Khalil. Thanks a fucking lot. If I had known you were going to tell everyone my business, I would have never asked for your help. I never needed you. I don't need you now. Way to be a really great friend." With that, I turn and leave. I don't want their stupid snacks. I want to go home. I want my bed and my dog. I slam the door, but Khalil catches it with his quick, strong arm and his cat like reflexes. "Yo. What the hell, Simone? What is wrong with you?" I said I was sorry. It's no big deal. Moriah is cool. So cool. She's not going to say anything. She wants to help. She's totally into it. Check your feed. See for yours..."

I stop him again. I don't know what I want to say though. She does seem cool and he's probably right about her not saying anything. That's not even why I'm upset. I've been wanting to tell everyone anyways. He has no idea why I'm mad and hurt. Before I can stop myself, I blurt out, "That's not it. That's not why I'm...I'm...," I am crying. AGAIN. Big gulps of tears. Snot is dripping from my nose. AGAIN. I run my forearms across my face like I'm four years old. I should go ahead and start stamping my feet and screaming. That's what I want to do anyways. "Why are you mad then, Simone? I don't know what you're doing right now. What is this?"

"I came here to give you a chance. To give us a chance. I came here to tell you that I think I probably love you or something. I thought you'd be excited. I thought you'd be happy." I'm starting to hiccup. A full on ugly cry. I don't think it's just this situation that has me wrecked; I think it is Langdon, Stephen, Axl, and now, the saddest part...my friend Khalil. I'm ruining things with my lifelong friend. A guy who would walk around a city trying to get a good signal to watch a medium dole out readings to strangers. And now I'm ruining everything. Our friendship. My shot at true love.

"You what? What? Now?" He comes closer to me and pulls me to him. "I can't believe this. If you had told me this a month ago, I would be doing back flips in the yard right now. Now I'm with Moriah though. She's dope as hell." He's incredulous but not sad. He's into her. I cry harder. This is not helping. He's warm and strong. He smells like forest. He keeps talking. He's shaking his head in disbelief. Shaking his head as if the movement will make all the pieces fall back into place.

"Simone, you told me no so many times. You told me never. I'm a real person with real feelings. I'm not gonna jump when you say jump. When we were younger, that was fine I guess. That was kids' stuff. But we're in high school now. I'm serious about having a girlfriend. I told you I would always be your friend, but I got needs. I want to take a girl to the movies and kiss her before, during, and after it. I want to buy her red hearts filled with chocolate and stuffed teddy bears on Valentine's Day. I want someone cheering me on at my matches, wearing my last name on the back of her shirt. You didn't want any of that. You made it clear. I made a choice to be happy, Simone. Don't be mad because I'm happy."

I struggle to catch my breath. It's coming in little shudders. I know he's right. I can't expect him to drop everything and suddenly be the thing I told him he'd never be. That's not fair. The Guilt Dragon swipes a claw across my heart. Now I'm afraid I'll lose my friend. I don't have a long line of them. "I don't expect you to drop everything," I manage to say. "I want us all to be happy. True love like Mrs. Carpenter said. I didn't mean to make things weird. I just thought it could work. All my other dates have sucked so bad and you're a good friend to me. Don't mind what I said earlier. Moriah seems awesome. I'm sorry." I don't really know what I'm apologizing for, but I need for this to be over. At the very least, I need things to be back the way they were ASAP.

On cue, Moriah appears in the doorway with water and a stack of Thin Mints. That's a perfect snack right there. She pretends not to notice the strange vibe or my snot-covered, tear-stained face. "Here you go, Simone. I hope you feel better. This heat though. Good for you for running. I take walks with my dog, but I'm not a runner." She even walks her dog. She hands me ice-cold water and a few tissues. She's good. I wipe my face off and take a long swig of water. I do feel better. Water is magic.

"You better now, Simone?" He's not just asking about the water.

"I'm fine. Yeah. Thanks. I gotta get going though. Lots to do. It's nice to meet you." I'm going for a nod but Moriah comes in for a full on squeeze.

"You too! I've been dying to meet THE Queen Canary. That's so awesome, what you're doing. All Saints is all in!"

"Thanks," I mumble out of surprising humility.

"Also, my sister really wants to meet you. She's the one that's deep into psychic stuff. I mostly just go along for the ride. Although my reading has worked out pretty well so far." She grins at Khalil and pokes his shoulder with her purple glittering fingernail. "She's on the track team. A runner like you. Not just a dog-walker like me." She laughs at herself. She has a big, loud laugh for a such a small person. It honks like a goose. It's the kind of laugh you'd expect out of someone who is 6 feet tall and can pick tires up over their head. But it suits her. That's the best part.

"Yeah, let's do that sometime soon," Khalil jumps in. "You'll love Melia. She's a bad-ass sprinter for sure. Actually you probably won't care anything about that but all her competition sure does." The boy and his sports. He's passionate you gotta give him that.

"Okay, sure I guess." Life without Connelly has taught me I should probably make a new friend or two for back-up. "I gotta go. See ya soon."

"Bye! Nice to meet you! Good luck with everything. We'll be at the pole on Thursday!" Moriah calls after me. Dang. She's nice.

CHAPTER NINETEEN

Wednesday, September 24

I feign physical sickness on Wednesday. My mom lets me stay home, but she's extremely worried about me. She knows I don't just have a stomachache. She knows there's more to how I'm feeling than I'm letting on. I need some time to myself. I know I can't take more than one day. Especially since we have the protest tomorrow. I know more than a few days of lying low and sleeping means I'm heading towards a dark place. It's a balance of rest and solitude to recharge but not so much that I get isolated. My mom makes sure I take my medication. She asks if I need an emergency visit with Dr. A. I say I do not. I can wait until Friday.

I've gotten nothing from Connelly. No calls. No texts. Kahlil sends me a few follow up texts all week saying how sorry he is that he told Moriah about Queen Canary. He hopes I won't be too mad. He knows it was wrong. He really wants us all to hang out. He thinks I'll really like her a lot. Isn't Moriah amazing? When do I want to meet Malia? I answer them all. I need for us to get back to the way we were immediately. One thing I keep thinking about is how I felt when he hugged me. I felt the way I always feel with Khalil. That he's warm and inviting and strong and sincere. It felt like any other quick hug we've had over the years. There was no spark. I expected to feel something different. Something shiny and pulsing since I'd decided I was going to love him like that. I didn't actually. I felt safe and loved, but not like the kind I was going for. I still feel heart-broken, but it's for everything. All the boys that haven't worked out. Not just for Khalil. Us not working out *like that* is probably for the best. Now I want to do anything to make him forget that I put us in that strange spot. Be normal.

Most of the morning I lay in bed and watch *New Girl* on Netflix. By lunchtime, I'm coming out of my funk. Jessica Day will do that to me every time. Plus I'm getting hungry. A good sign I'm taking care of myself and am not going to spiral. Before I go downstairs to make my new favorite vegetarian meal, bean burritos with guacamole and salsa, I check the email account I set up for Queen Canary. Two important and exciting things. One, the journalist that I reached out to emails me back. I am giddy at the sight of his name in my inbox.

Dear Queen Canary,

Hello. I've been following your work. It's fantastic. Way to go! The world is listening. I'd love to be a part of your movement. I have many ideas for the kinds of articles that I can write. The first one will be a scathing expose on the whole conspiracy. I'm ready to call out some big names and demand they admit to what they have done and figure out how to make up for it. I read the report when you first posted it. I've already begun working with the school that is nearest to me. I interviewed several kids today as well as teachers and the principal. I've written to the school board but haven't heard back yet. I have permission from my editor to run the article tomorrow morning. That's great timing as you'll be running your protests. It will be a big bang! My editor is also committed to keep running stories as long as it takes. She says this is critically important to our readers. Since we are right here in D.C. and The Post serves the metro area, it will get the attention of our government officials as well as the nation. Consider it done and done! It's going to be an excellent move in the right direction. I'll send you an advanced copy tonight. We're in this together. I'd love to meet you when you're ready. Another article in the series can be about you. You deserve it. This is great work.

Yours in Truth,

VLWJ

Vance Lewis-Marker Jr.

Sr. Columnist

The Post

Yes! This is exactly what the movement needs. I can't wait to read the article and see what happens. I write him back and thank him for everything. I thank him on behalf of The Flock. It's nice of him to acknowledge that this is hard work. I agree, but I didn't do the work of the school conspiracy report. How did I get that? Who did that work? That person or group of people also deserves some credit once all this is sorted out. I need to figure out who @undercoverearthmom1965 is.

The other piece of good news is from my dad. He filed the paperwork and we are good to go for a full on rally on Sunday, September 28th. We have a permit to house it on The Mall. Dad sends me a link and reminds me to do my research so that I stay in bounds. No need to cause extra trouble. I look through all of the rules and regulations and then begin a campaign to promote

The Mother Earth March on Sunday, September 28th on The Mall. Come one, Come all. Bring your signs, banners, friends, families, chants, and more. Show D.C. what you love about Earth. Show them why it matters that she thrives. Tell them what to stop doing. Tell them what to start doing. Let's be the change. When I'm done (for now), I jump around my room. I don't feel at all sad or depressed right now. Right now, I feel powerful and strong. I feel like I can take on the world. No one can stop me and everyone can help me.

CHAPTER TWENTY

Thursday, September 26

It's Flock This Thursday and even though I feel wrung out from the emotion of the past couple of days and there's a hole in my heart where Connelly should be, I'm still excited about the protest. I'm up before the jingle of my alarm. I get ready quickly, well, I get ready like I always do, which is quickly. Today's vintage T of the day is one I asked my mom to buy me online a few days ago. It arrived last night. It's white with the traditional blue and green Earth in the background. In the foreground, all are the animals you can think of dotting the sky and oceans of the world. It's straight-up 90's. The colors are muted and warm. The art is realistic. Another irritating reminder that we have known about this shit for a while now and still haven't done anything about it. My jeans are bell-bottoms, unfortunately not original. I still can't manage one long braid down my back, but I cobble together two-side braids that stop at my shoulders once my hair is wound together. Black Chucks. Concealer on Gertrude. She's placed herself squarely in the middle of my pointy chin. Damn you, Gertrude. I head downstairs lugging the poster-sized pictures of Cherry Garcia, mom, dad, Longview High, and Connelly.

As I get ready, I check my phone. Still nothing from Connelly. I sigh. It makes me so sad. I'm upset that we are fighting, but I'm also upset about what she said to me. She knows me better than that, right? There are more texts from Khalil. He's still persistent, I see.

Flagpole pictures are already rolling in from the East Coast. Students are carrying pictures and posters of everything they love. I'm smiling like the Cheshire Cat right now. So big. It's weird to be so sad for myself but so happy for something bigger than me. It's strange that the mind and body can hold so many different feelings at once.

My parents are eating granola at the table. It's too early to leave. They make me sit down and eat. We talk about our plan for the morning. Finally, they agree it's the right time to leave and we make our way to school. I've convinced my mom not to mom so hard and to let the kids bring what they need on their own. I'm also hoping to not draw any more attention to myself than necessary. Not yet anyways. I rub the rabbit's foot as we walk towards the school building. Sending out hopeful wishes for a good crowd. On the walk to campus (stepping over all the cracks), we are not the only people heading to school. I count at least ten other families walking to school with us. My phone buzzes in my pocket. A text from Khalil.

we out here!!!

yo mad ppl @ pole

way more than last time

lots of adults tho

He sends the teeth gritting emoji with that last message. He also sends a pic of him holding a picture of himself, Connelly, and me. It was taken a few summers ago when our families went camping together. We're standing in front of a huge gorgeous waterfall. The water is rough and white behind us. The sky is Carolina Blue. We are smiling and waving peace signs at the camera. Cherry Garcia at our feet.

u r a good friend

thx

post more pics, tag me

have a good day

I don't know what else to do. He is sorry. He's in love with Moriah. She may be his girlfriend, but he is my true friend. It's hard to grieve what you didn't lose. I didn't lose my friend. My friend gained happiness, and true love it seems. That's good news for my plan, I figure. Can't hurt. I'm also learning you can be happy and sad at the same time. Even about the same thing. It doesn't mean my heart doesn't hurt, it does. It actually feels sore in my chest. I smile though. A thin, mixed-up feeling kind of smile.

My smile turns into laughter that pours out of me when I turn the corner. There are people everywhere. The front lawn is full of parents, teachers, staff, students, dogs, posters, signs, banners, and more. The things and people that people love are plastered on their posters, their t-shirts, or they brought them with them. Families came together. They brought their pets. They brought symbols of the things they love. One many is carrying a Virginia Tech helmet. One girl is carrying the Swim Team's State Championship trophy. Someone's carrying a cross. Someone else brings a model of volcano, like from their 4th grade science project. A kid from my pre-cal class is waving around a map the size of a smart car. There are a large number of globes too. Well done, friends. Well done. There's an odd lady who lives down the road from me who brought a cat on a leash. You do you. My mom reaches over and squeezes my shoulder. She gives me a wink and a smile. It feels good.

I also notice a few other things that are different today. There are five or so police officers roaming the crowd. Their patrol cars parked along the perimeter of the school. The sirens are off, but the blue lights are on. There is also a local news crew. Yes! Thank you, universe. A reporter is walking around interviewing the peaceful protestors. Things are going well.

Very well. I check my phone to see what's going on at the other schools. Same thing. Crowds are bigger. Signs are full of loved items and people and places and things. It's a beautiful sight. We just need a certain someone to take notice already. Ahem. Ahem.

I make my way to the reporter. I don't want to seem overly eager. No need to cause any suspicion. I just want to hear what people are saying. I lug the picture poster of Longview High with me. I want the connection to be clear that what we are protesting here is because of the school conspiracy and climate change. We're not out here just to skip class; we are here to make a difference. Using kids and schools as pawns to make money, make kids sick, and make climate change worse is not okay. We're not here for it. A reporter is interviewing a boy from my Spanish class.

"Tell us why you are here today," the reporter says to him.

Calvin (I think that's his name) clearly states, "I'm here because I've been worried about the climate crisis for a while now, and I'm upset about it." He rubs his chin. I don't know what he's rubbing because his face is as bare as a baby's butt, but nonetheless. He is gravely serious though, I'll give him that. He goes on, "When I learned about the school conspiracy from @queencanary and The Flock, I became very upset. It was really upsetting to know that the government doesn't care about all kids and that money and greed and power are more important than a healthy planet and healthy students." He stops speaking and looks at the reporter for a signal for what to do next. She asks him another question.

"What impact do you think this protest will have?"

"Mam, I'm not sure about this particular protest here at LHS, but there's also a petition with thousands and thousands of signatures. I'm not sure if you know this yet, mam, but there are protests like this happening all over the country this morning. Kids are really tired of this....*stuff*. We want it to stop. We want reform. We want the government to acknowledge what they are doing and to do better. We want them to make all this stuff that's wrong, well, right, I guess." He raises his eyebrows for more direction.

"Is that so?" she asks. "Well, isn't that so very enterprising of you all." She looks at the camera straight on and says, "Well, there you have it, Longview. These kids are apparently fed up with what they call the climate crisis and the school conspiracy. As you can see, there are hundreds of people protesting here at Longview High School this morning. I'm sure the team here at Channel 7, just as enterprising as these young people, will have an update for you at the mid-day newscast. That's all for now, reporting live from Longview High School, home of the Lions. We hope you have a roar of a day!"

I roll my eyes. Lame. I'm intrigued by the mid-day update though. The more the merrier. The reporter hands her mic to her cameraman. They turn to leave. "Ms. Uhh..Ms. Re..Reporter..." God. Clearly her name is not Ms. Reporter, but I have no idea what it is. She is kind enough to turn around and address me, now the super lame one. "Yes?" She's polite but ready to leave. That's evident. "Hi. Um, Yeah, I am just wondering why you're here?" That came out wrong. "I'm sorry. I mean, like how did you know to come here this morning?" She looks at me evenly. "I follow Queen Canary. Like everyone else in this town. Time's up for this...stuff...as that kid said. I'm with you guys." She turns and walks away.

I stop in my tracks. Everyone in this town? It's easier to think about @queencanary as something not here, not in my hometown. Maybe because I have been anonymous. It's cool though that the people in my town are part of The Flock. I'm grinning from ear to ear when I feel a large, heavy hand on my shoulder. It stops me mid-step. I turn around slowly. I'm cringing already. I have a feeling I know who it is. And, I'm right. Principal Aguilera. "I need to speak with you, Ms. Marker. I asked that you come to my office earlier in the week. I haven't seen you yet." I scan the area around the flagpole in search of my parents, but I can't locate them in the crowd. Too many bodies, too many signs. "Okay. Sorry about that. It's been a busy week with school and all. I stayed at home sick yesterday too." "Yes, I'm sure it's been a very busy week for you, Ms. Marker. In so many ways. I need to ask you a few questions." "Okay." I say again. Stay neutral. Stay normal. Be normal. Breezy. Be more like Connelly, less like Simone.

"For one thing, I want to make sure you are okay. Some of the chaperones at the dance said that when you left, you looked very upset. They said you ran away from the gym. Is everything okay, Ms. Marker?" I'm so surprised by this act of kindness and genuine concern that I am speechless. I stare at him blankly for too many moments. He repeats himself. "Ms. Marker, are you okay? Was everything okay at the dance?" I gather myself. "Yes, yes. I'm fine, sir. Everything is fine. I just had a tiny argument with my best friend. It caught me off guard that's all. I probably overreacted." "One of the chaperones followed you, but said you disappeared from the street before she could catch up with you. She said it looked like perhaps someone approached you. She couldn't make everything out in the darkness."

Oh, shit. I never thought about someone seeing Axl and me. "Um, yes. I'm fine. I just ran home pretty quickly. I was just ready to be at home, ya know." "I see. Ms. Marker, student safety is very important to me. Even after the school day ends. OR in this case, before school starts."Although technically we are well in to first block right now. He continues talking, "Ms. Marker, last week I came on the PA system and made an announcement the organizer of these protests. I made it clear that our school is a peaceful place for learning. For learning as much as we can. I want you to know that I think what is happening today is excellent learning. I'm not supposed to say that nor can I be visibly supportive of protests and gathering such as this on school property, but I'm telling you." I gulp or at least I try to gulp but my throat is so dry I can't. I don't know where this is going. "So, why are you telling me?" "Security cameras, Ms. Marker. They are all over the school and the entire campus." Oh, shit. "I, uh, my mom an..." He interrupts me.

"Ms. Marker, listen. I have known that you were the on campus ringleader since before I made that announcement this week. I have to do what I have to per my responsibilities as the principal of this school. That said, I will protect you. I can tell this means a lot to you, and it means a lot to me too. I read the report. I'm as mad as you are. Keep doing what you need to do. I'll keep doing what I have to do. Good day, Ms. Marker."

I'm left standing on the sidewalk looking over the front lawn. Part shocked, part relieved, part motivated. I need to do more. I have room to do more at school. Principal Aguilera didn't say anything about Queen Canary; he thinks I'm just the school leader. Fine by me. For now. I take out my phone and Tweet out a picture from my perch above all of LHS.

> *What's love got to do with it?*

#everything #findtruelove #reform #schoolconspiracy #climatecrisis #flockthisthursday #youngandwild #birdseyeview

Let's see what The Flock will do with that. I also remind everyone to sign the petition. I shove my phone back in my pocket and join the group. A chant rises up from the crowd. The hour is nearly up, but these little Flockers are chanting, "Heck no, we won't go. Heck no, we won't go." This isn't exactly what I had in mind, but nothing terrible is happening. We aren't being violent. We're here to protest making the world a better place. A place where we can all actually live. The chant is loud and big. It vibrates between bodies and gains momentum. Principal Aguilera is at the flagpole with a bullhorn.

"Students, it is time to go back to class. It's time to get back to learning. I repeat, it is time to go back to class. In an orderly fashion, please make your way back to class." The only people who can actually here him are near him and his bullhorn. The students are chanting louder now. Before I know what's happening, the police officers turn their sirens on and begin moving their cars around and through the protestors. Quickly, we move out of their way. They aren't going fast just methodical like a Zamboni machine, sweeping us away like shards of ice. No one is in danger. It just forces everyone to move inside the building. I don't like it, but I'm not freaking out about it. But somebody is.

Someone is screaming my name. I can't place the voice. I look around. I'm trying to figure out where my name is coming from. I spot a girl from Connelly's Visual Arts class. Sometimes she eats lunch with us. Veronica Lyles. Why is Veronica Lyles screaming my name? I'm so disoriented, but my body reacts more quickly that my brain. I run towards Veronica who is kneeling beside Connelly. Connelly. My Connelly. Connelly is curled up in a ball on the sidewalk where the police cars were lined up earlier. Did someone hit her? Is she hurt? Did she get run over? As I run, I yell for my mom. I have no idea where she is. I just yell for her and hope her Mom-Power kicks in and she senses that I need her to find me. She's a nurse and will know what to do.

When I get to Veronica and Connelly, I am screaming. "What's wrong? What happened?" Cries catch in my throat. I can't let another bad thing happen to her on my account. Veronica grabs my shoulders and looks me in the face. "Calm down, Simone. Be calm. I don't know what's wrong with her but you yelling and screaming is not helping." She's right. I take a deep breath. I bend down next to her. "Connelly, talk to me. What's wrong? What happened?" I look at her more closely. It looks like she's hyperventilating. Something I'm familiar with.

"Get me some sort of bag. Like a paper bag." I say it loud

and clear. I don't want to scare her, but I need someone to hear me and listen. There's so much noise in the background. Some kids still chant, the police sirens wail, and Principal Aguilera is still on the stupid bull horn. It's so freaking stressful.

"Connelly. I'm here. I'm here. Me. Simone. You're going to be okay. Try to breathe deeply. Try to get some air to your brain. Everything is going to be okay." I text my mom to help us. I tell her where we are. Then I lay down bedside Connelly. I keep talking to her. "Connelly. Help is coming. My mom is coming. My mom and dad are here. They are going to help you. It's ok. Try to breathe. I love you. I'm so sorry we've been fighting." Shit. I don't mean to bring that up. She doesn't need more things to be upset about right now. I think she's having a panic attack. There's no blood or anything. She doesn't look hurt. She looks stressed, sad, anxious, angry, overwhelmed, lonely, and scared. She's sweating and shaking a little bit but not too bad. Where is my mom? She's holding herself like she's cold even though it's unnaturally warm for late September. Global warming. I feel so bad for her. I continue to lay by her and talk to her. It's only been a few minutes, maybe three, but it feels like so much longer. She still can't catch her breath.

Then my mom. My god-blessed mom. She's on the scene and clearing away the silly people who are gathered around Connelly like she's a circus act. My mom lifts Connelly up and helps her sit on the curb. She talks to her softly. She even manages a light chuckle. She's smoothing her hair and holding her hand. My mom is awesome. It's another full five minutes before Connelly is breathing normally again. She's still not talking, but she's catching her breath. She's not shaking anymore, but her face is still damp and clammy looking. A few more minutes pass. My mom just keeps being awesome. She gets Connelly to drink water she pulls from her purse. Mom's gotta mom. I sit beside Connelly and mimic what my mom does. My dad jogged home to get the car. He pulls up and we put Connelly in the backseat and drive her to our house.

At our house, my mom settles us in the living room with snacks and a movie, like we are in first grade again. I like it. Connelly still hasn't said anything, which is really weird. Other than that though, she seems better. My mom is talking to Mr. Carpenter on the phone. I hear mom reassuring him that everything is okay. She retells what she knows. She explains the protest, the noise, the police, the chanting, and the crowd. She also speculates that Connelly was likely triggered by the content of the protest since we can now safely assume that the school conspiracy contributed to Mrs. Carpenter's death. She explains that Connelly had a mild panic attack and that she's resting comfortably at our house. I notice she doesn't say anything about Connelly not actually speaking yet. She's very reassuring.

Mr. Carpenter says he will get there as soon as he can, but he's about to step into an important meeting with President Robinson and some other big wigs. I give my mom The Look and she assures him that we will take great care of Connelly and that he should take his time. I will him to fall in love with the President and for her to fall in love with him and for them all to agree on how to fix everything wrong with the world in this one meeting. How hard could it be?

I sit close to Connelly on the couch. I don't say anything right away. I'm hoping when she's ready she'll talk to me. I have so many questions. I want to know what happened and if she hates me. I want to know why she said those things to me at the dance. I want to know why she's upset. I want to know what she thinks about my letter. We sit in silence for several minutes. *Lilo and Stitch* plays in the background. Mom must have felt like were in first grade too. Cherry Garcia lies between us snoring softly. Finally, I can't take it anymore.

"Connelly, what's going on? With you? With us? Everything?" I want to reach for her hand but I don't. I don't want us to be mad at each other anymore, but I don't know where we stand. She doesn't say anything for a full minute. I'm worried maybe she can't talk anymore or maybe she can't hear me. Its an unnatural silence. Finally she begins, and it all comes out. "I'm not exactly sure what happened at school today. I just got overwhelmed and sad and anxious. It was so loud. I couldn't hear myself think. I was so mad too. About everything. The state of the world. The government. My mom. Zach. My dad. You. I want to do something. I want to help. I want justice for my mom and for any kid out there who is sick or lost someone because of this mess. It's so much though, you know? Like where do you start? Will it be enough? Will it make a difference? How can one girl in Virginia do anything about the climate crisis all over the world." Don't I know it. Story of my life. I just nod, encouraging her to keep talking.

"Once that poster was put up at school, I did some research into mom's cancer, into our school, into the climate crisis-like what you were talking about in your dream. I'm scared for all of us. And today, with all that noise and all those people, I guess I just like freaked out. I couldn't take it all." Again. Don't I know it. Story of my life. "You're okay now though, right?"

"I guess. Like for the moment. I can breathe. I don't feel like I'm dying or having a heart attack. That's an improvement. It just feels like I've been holding so much inside for so long. Trying to be strong. Trying to be happy. But it's so hard. And well, things are just not that great or maybe they are fine, they just aren't easy. Not like they used to me. When we were younger. When my mom was still here." I nod some more. She's right. Growing up kinda sucks. I think about Khalil and how easy it used to be. Now it's more complicated. Losing something you never had hurts. I think about how bad it must hurt to lose what Connelly has lost.

"I'm sorry for what I said to you at the dance. Like I said, things have been hard and I've not been dealing with them very well. I guess I've been kind of mad at you for a while but I don't really even know why. I can't exactly explain it. And then your dream and everything. Plus all the conspiracy stuff at school. It's all been bringing up all these feelings about my mom. I've been really confused and upset. I'm not used to feeling those ways. I took it out on you. I'm sorry. I'm really sorry for what I said. I'm so sorry." Her voice cracks. A tear walks its way down and around the apple of her cheek. "I forgive you. I've already forgiven you." I have more to say, but she keeps talking. "And Zach is being kind of an ass. I don't know what's up with him. Or us. That's one of the reasons I was upset at the dance. I wasn't happy being with him that night. I haven't been happy with him a lot lately." This is bad for my true love plans for Connelly, but I'm relieved to hear her say this. Zach has been giving me bad vibes too...for a while.

"I don't like how he was acting when he was drinking. I think he's been lying to me about where he is and what he's doing. And it's hard because he wants to do all this physical stuff. I like it actually. It feels good. I don't feel lonely when we're together like that. But he wants more from me than I think I'm ready for. He puts a lot of pressure on me. I think I want to break up with him, but he's going to be really mad. I don't want that either. But then some days I think there's no way I want to break up with him because he can also be really nice. That's crazy. How can I feel so differently about him day to day?" She stops talking. I can tell this is hard for her. She's never said anything about Zach. She's never told me any of this. In my short dating life, I can attest to the confusion. How one minute you can feel one way and the next moment you feel the complete opposite.

"Well, one thing I've learned lately is that my feelings about someone change based on how they act. So if he's acting like a jerk, then you're not going to be feeling all that great about him. It's easier to feel happy about someone when they are being nice. If your feelings are changing that much, it's probably because he's changing that much. That's unfair to you. You deserve to be with someone you feel good about all the time. He doesn't deserve you if he's not nice to you." She's crying now. "You're so awesome, Connelly. You're so kind and cheerful. Always to everyone. But you haven't been yourself at all lately. I'm worried about you. Dump him. You deserve so much more."

"There's more," she says. "I think my dad might be dating someone." My ears perk up. "You do?" I also feel the Guilt Dragon slice my insides. Although I realize that she's not said anything about my letter. If she'd read my letter she would know all the things that I have to be sorry for. She would know that possibly her dad was dating someone because of me. She would know about Queen Canary and how all my work has upset her and caused her to have a panic attack at school in front of most of our student body and the town. She didn't read my letter. If she had, she might be even more upset. She might not have asked for me to forgive her. I'm not sure what to do. That's not true. I know what I need to do. I need to come clean. I need to tell her the whole truth. But she's not through pouring out her soul. I don't talk yet.

"I mean, I guess it makes sense. I guess it's time. I just. I wish he would at least be honest with me about it. He's sneaking around. He says he's working late a lot. I'm sure he is, I guess. I know his job is really important. I know that now more than ever. If he's going to have a girlfriend, or whatever adults call them, I'd at least like to meet her. I think I do anyways. Maybe I'll freak out though like I did today." She tries to laugh but it doesn't really come out right. It's not really funny. Mental health and all. She seems to have gotten out most of what she needs to say. I need to tell her everything.

"Con, did you get the letter I put in your locker?"

"Letter? What letter?" I guess that's a no. "I wrote you a letter. I, uh, have to tell you some things. I put it in your locker. You didn't see it?" "No, have you seen the inside of my locker? I'm surprised you could even fit a piece of paper in there. I don't know why I have so much stuff at school. Have you ever noticed my book bag? It's like fifty pounds of notebooks and paper and my camera. My back hurts." She's at least laughing a little now, but probably not for long. I tell her everything. I start at the beginning at the Sixth Sense Conference. I am nervous to tell her about the message from her mom, but I do. She cries. She cries hard. I stop and let her. I cry too. I tell her how hard I'm working to forgive myself and to make up for what I've done.

"So, that might be why your dad is dating. I've been wishing for it and asking the universe for him to..." I hesitate, "to like fall in love with the President and for her to fall in love with him too." She looks at me like I'm crazy and bursts out laughing. She's laughing so hard, she has to run to the bathroom because she's peeing her pants a little. She comes back into the room and throws herself on the couch beside me.

"Simone, of all the things you've ever said about your powers and your pre-whatever it's called, that is by far my favorite. I don't think you need to worry about making my dad fall in love with the President. I am definitely not mad because that is insane. You are hilarious." She sits up and is more serious now that her uncontrollable giggles have subsided. "Also, I do want my dad to be happy. And I trust you. If my mom said that we should all find true love, then we should. I don't have that with Zach. I just don't. I need to break up with him. But I have you."

"What do you mean?" I'm confused by her statement.

"Simone, you are my best friend. We have literally been through the worst and the best things in life together. I love you. Our friendship is the truest love of all. Don't you think?" She punches my arm playfully.

"Well, yeah, I mean. I never thought of it like that, but yes." A huge smile takes over my face. My thin non-glossed lips showing how happy I am at this realization. "Yes, Connelly! You are so right. Why didn't I think of that? I've been so worried about boys and dating and layers," I tug at my hair to show my disdain, "I never thought about it like that," I say again. "We are true love. Me and you." I'm so relieved at this epiphany. I don't have to go on any more dates. I don't have to deal with any more Axls. I need to tell Connelly about Axl and Khalil. I assume she knows about Moriah. *Murchae, Chlo*

"Connelly, something bad happened when I left the dance." I tell her about Axl. I tell her the good parts. The kissing. I even tell her about how he touched me. I somehow get out the words about how I liked it some of it. I can't believe I'm saying these words out loud. She's nodding though. She says she understands. That's how physical stuff can complicate things like with Zach. The more body parts you have involved the more complicated it gets. We agree. I tell her about how he wanted me to touch him and how I didn't want to. That he kept putting my hands on him and how I hated that part of it. It's my turn to cry again. I tell her how violated I felt, how angry and ashamed I am. I tell her how badly she hurt my feelings and then Axl turns around and hurts me in different way. Connelly feels terrible about this. She gets a visit from the Guilt Dragon. I assure her it isn't her fault. We can't let the bad decisions of boys become the burden of each other or ourselves. What Axl did, Axl did on his own accord. Was I upset? Yes. Was Connelly mean to me? Yes. Does that mean we should take responsibility for Axl? No. We hug. And cry. And realize how fortunate we are to have each other no matter what. This is what true love looks like and it looks amazing on us.

I tell her about Khalil and how I thought I might like him for more than a friend. She knows about Moriah and I can see her heart breaking for mine. She also looks a little grossed out. I guess the thought of her bestie and her cousin is a little much for her to get her head around right now. She doesn't have to though. I tell her about when I went over there and how stupid I felt. How embarrassed I was. I also tell her how happy I am for him and we agree that Moriah is "dope as hell" as he describes her. I tell her that I'm mad at him because he told Moriah that I'm Queen Canary.

"What?" she interrupts me. "Did you just say you are

Queen Canary? Like on the socials? With thousands upon thousands of followers? Like planning protests and stuff?" She's staring at me. Astonished. I nod slowly. I can't tell if she thinks this is a good or a bad thing. I know the content of Queen Canary is upsetting to her. She's made that clear. I need to make sure she knows I'm doing it for her, for her mom, for her dad, for all of us. "Oh my god, Simone. Shut up. You are not. That is awesome. I'm so proud of you. You are changing the world. I've been following everything. It's hard to see. It hurts my heart. Don't get me wrong, but I'm learning so much. I know things got crazy this morning, but it's really amazing, Simone." I tell her that I posted a picture of this morning's protest from my @queencanary accounts, so it may just be a matter of time before I'm figured out or I come clean. "Let's do it right now. Let's do a video." "And then what? What will that accomplish? I have to have a plan. This has gotten big." We talk about The Mother Earth March planned for The Mall. I explain why I'm doing it, so that President Robinson can't miss it. She'll have to pay attention. "Did you notice that she can see the whole mall from her office?"

"Um, no. I barely remember anything. I was so star struck."

"So, you didn't notice that I left your dad's phone number and call me on a sticky note?" I ask with some trepidation. "You did what?" She's laughing again hysterically. "You think that a Post-it is going to get the President to fall in love with him? You're an idiot. A cute idiot." I blush. It wasn't my best idea, but it was all I could come up with five minutes notice. We talk and talk and talk. We get it all out. It feels so good. She's so right. We do have true love. I have it too with Khalil. I have it with my parents and Cherry Garcia. I have so much love in life. I'm spoiled with it.

We open up Twitter to see how the protests are going. There are thousands of pictures from schools all over the East Coast and the middle of the country. They are showing all the things they love. My heart fills up completely. How could adults in charge of things not see how much there is to fight for? How can they not get their act together? When you combine all the science facts with all the emotions of the heart, isn't this a no-brainer? I think about President Robinson. What is keeping her from believing? I can't figure it out. We like as many posts as we can and retweet hundreds. We are laughing and talking. There are no more secrets between us. We're back. We're true love. I've always had it. Connelly and Simone. Conn and SAM. Maybe the old wacky lady at the conference wasn't so wacky after all.

My mom comes in and says that we have visitors. She looks at our red noses and bloodshot eyes; we did a lot of crying. She suggests we run upstairs and freshen up just a bit. "Mooo-ooom. Seriously why? Who is here?"

"Simone Alice Marker. Go upstairs and freshen up right now. This is not a request; it is an order. I'm serious." Connelly catches my eye and shrugs. It's not worth a fight I guess. Upstairs I wash my face and smooth out my hair. Connelly cleans up the mascara streaks off her face. "Why is my mom being so weird right now?" "You're lucky to have her." Words of wisdom in a regretful tone from my best friend. I shut up and nod. When we are presentable, we go back downstairs. Nothing my mom could have said would have prepared me for what I saw when we walked into the living room. Sitting side-by-side, *holding hands*, are Mr. Carpenter and the President of the United States of America.

"Connelly!" Mr. Carpenter jumps up and takes three giant steps to get to Connelly quickly. He scoops her up in a bear hug, lifting her off the ground. "You're okay. You're okay." He murmurs over and over gain. "I was so worried. I got here as fast as I could. The President was nice enough to reschedule our meeting. Family first. You're okay. You're okay." He's rambling. His voice full of love and worry. "Daddy. You're squeezing me too tightly." Connelly says, and she's also crying again. "Oh my heavens. I'm so sorry. I've just been so worried about you. Not only today but for weeks and I didn't know what to do or to say.

I thought it was too late to help you. You haven't been yourself. I'm so sorry. I'm so sorry." The words are tumbling out now. He might not have known what to say, but he's making up for it. "You've seemed so sad, and well-I've been so much happier." He scans the room for the President. "And I've been feeling so guilty about..." He stops talking for a moment, realizing what he's about to confess. Realizing that we already know now. Also, the Guilt Dragon doesn't quit. He goes after everyone. He puts Connelly down gently and reaches for her two hands. He puts them in his. "Connelly, I'm so sorry for not telling you this before. It's only been a week or so that I knew exactly what to say but haven't said it. Connelly, The President, uh, Naomi, and I, well, we, I think we're in love."

It is taking everything in my whole body to not jump for joy, although that is all I want to do. I did it. Connelly and I have each other. Her dad and the President have each other. Shoot, even Khalil found true love. I grin wildly. I can't help that, but at least my two feet stay on the ground. I search Connelly's face for her reaction. I have no idea what she will think about this. Will she be the First Step-daughter? Is that a thing? Connelly is nodding ever head ever so slightly. Mr. Carpenter keeps speaking, for better or for worse. "You see, we've been working together day and night to figure out a lot of things that need changing. We've spent so much time together. We've had many deep talks about what we believe and why we believe it. We've argued. We've rarely agreed, actually." His voice is matter-of-fact and warm. He looks for confirmation from the President. I'm not sure I can refer to her as Naomi quite yet. She looks back at him with what looks like love if you ask me, but I'm no expert. Her gaze is steady, strong, and kind. She encourages him with a nod.

"We've discussed everything from religion to our childhoods to favorite take-out, to the environment and how to protect it. We've learned so much about each other. There are so many things that I love about Naomi, but there are two things that are most important. I want to make sure that you know these things about her, Connelly." He is completely dialed in to Connelly. It's intense.

"She knows how much I loved and love your mother. She knows that she was my world. I've shared with her the intensity and purity of our love and our marriage. She respects that. She respects the perfection that was your mom. How good she was to both of us. How good she was to her students and her community. She knows that she's irreplaceable when it comes to the memories and the life the three of us had together. She understands because she experienced a similar loss. She can really empathize."

The conversation is so intimate and special. I'm not sure I should still be in the room, but I also don't want to break the spell by saying something mundane like, *Excuse me. I'm going to get a pudding cup. Would anyone like one?* So, I just stand there still as a statue, trying to blend in with the living room furniture. I watch Connelly. She's frozen expect for her nearly imperceptible head nodding. She said that she thought her dad might be dating, so maybe the only real shock is who he is dating. It's pretty damn shocking even to me who has been planting little seeds and leaving little notes and begging the universe to intervene. She doesn't seem upset, just processing. I think that is what Dr. A would say.

He keeps going. "The second thing is, she really, really cares about people and the planet. She wants to do the right thing. She is open to change and learning. We discovered some pretty horrible things that have been occurring without her consent or knowledge through the school conspiracy classified report leak, which led us to investigate certain people and systems. People close to the President have been lying to her and manipulating the data they give her. She suspected that might be happening and that's why she brought me in. We actually worked together a long time ago on a city project. Technically, we've known each other for almost thirty years. I had forgotten. I guess I made quite the impression." He looks triumphant

183

at his own statement about himself. "We just haven't ever been personally close. She said she knew she could trust me to set her and these other crooks straight.

Once the school conspiracy report came out, it confirmed her suspicions and gave me and others specifics to investigate. It's going to take some time to unwind what has been done. It's also a very particular process due to well, politics. We are also under a tight timeline given the presidential debates are under way. We need to get ready to make a big splash. And, that's why she's here. When she heard about where you were this morning and the stance you and others are taking, everything that happened, and why I had to come to you, she wanted to be here with me to check on you. She also wants to say some things. Would you be okay with that? Do you need a minute? Are you okay? I'm sorry, I've been talking so much. So much has been happening." He looks from Connelly to The President. His nervous energy fills the room. He laughs to clear the air. The President is waiting patiently. Still and respectful on the couch giving them their space. I'm still standing there like a weirdo. "Connelly?"

She takes a big breath and lets it out slowly. Maybe I'm rubbing off on her. "Daddy, I want you to be happy. I miss mom, every day, but I know you do too. I know I can't replace mom and I know you can't either. To me, it is something neither of us would ever do. I'm not worried about that. I know you won't try to make her memory disappear I know that, Daddy. I also need you and me to keep her memory alive, like we have to purposely do that. I need to talk about her more with you." She chokes up just a little bit, but she's resolute. Her dad nods at her in agreement. That's all she needs to keep going. I supposed he already knows he should have been doing more of that.

"It's still a lot to take in. I'm going to need some time, I think. I've already been considering that you might be dating because you've been kind of sneaky and quiet and out late a lot. Which is fine, I'm not mad. I just sort of guessed already. I just didn't know it would be, like her. No offense." She looks The President in the eye when she says this. I think that's brave. She continues talking but directs her words to The President. "My dad is my whole life. From what I see on TV, you're not always that nice. You can't hurt him again. He's already had the worst hurts. I can't watch him be hurt again. I'm not sure that I trust you yet. It is going to take some time for me. It's not really like me to speak to adults this way, but one thing I'm learning about myself is that I need to be more open with my real feelings. I can't just nod and agree and look happy all the time. Apparently that doesn't work well after a while." She looks around the room to indicate the morning we've had. But if you came here to say some things, then that is fine. I can listen. I need to sit down though." She takes me by the hand and leads me to the love seat. I obediently sit next to her and keep hold of her hand. She gives permission with her eyes for The President to speak. Who is this bad-ass girl? I like it! I can't wait to hear what The President says.

"Hello, Connelly. It is nice to see you again. I am glad to see you are feeling better." She looks at me. "Hello, Simone. Thank you for having me at your home." I smile a small smile. It's not like she really gave me a choice or like I invited her, but I am thrilled she's here so it's fine. "Ladies, I am here for a couple of reasons. One, I want to apologize to you and every young person for not doing a good job protecting you. I have failed you so far, and for that I am very sorry. I intend to make it up to you and your generation and future generations as best I can. Lies and criminals blinded me from seeing the truth about the science of unnatural climate change and the state of the planet. I made very bad decisions based on the corrupt information I was fed. I did more damage to our Earth than I knew. That is an awful thing when you are a person who has the power to make the world a better place rather than a worse one. I am very ashamed of the impact that I have had so far." She takes a deep breath. Even The President has to breathe, I guess.

"Since I replaced many of my former staff, including the person who had the role your dad now does, I have been conducting my own research. I have used many sources and many experts. I have also been an active observer in some recent online activity. I want to perhaps ask you girls if you know anything about an online campaign aimed at getting my attention regarding the severity of the climate crisis. Would it be okay if I ask some perhaps presumptuous questions?" I don't even know what presumptuous means, but I don't think we really have a choice. We nod in unison. It feels good to be back in sync. "Okay, wonderful. Thank you, girls. I could be way off base, and if I am then you can redirect me. I have a theory though that I would like to run by you." She checks in again with us and we nod for her to go on.

"Okay, then. Well, first of all. We have many cameras that survey the White House. As you can imagine, safety is a priority." Oh shit. Why don't I ever think about cameras everywhere? I think I can see where this might be going. "After I met you both in my office a few weeks ago, I began noticing Post-it notes strewn about the White House. Nearly all of them were signed @queencanary." Connelly cuts me a look that could kill. I don't make eye contact. I pretend to be captivated by what The President is saying. She continues, "The facts on the Post-its were quite compelling. I looked up @queencanary as part of my research. I had a lot to sort out for myself after having been lied to and manipulated for so long. I found @queencanary to be very helpful. The account posted many curious facts, figures, predictions, and pictures. They led me to other sites, articles, and experts. I had so many questions, which often led to long conversations with this lovely man." Her seriousness cracks open when she looks at and speaks of Mr. Carpenter. It is pretty adorable.

"I learned even more from him. I trust him." She smiles at him. Then she turns her attention to us. "About the same time I, or my staff, was finding the @queencanary notes, I also found a similar note in my office. It was different in content and it was signed by, supposedly, Drew. He and I talked about it. Laughed about it and actually had a proper date because of it." Connelly's stare burns a hole in my head. I do not look at her. I work on keeping my face normal. Be normal. "I began putting two and two together. The timing. Who had access to what and when, et-cetera. I am wondering if one of you, specifically Simone, might be @queencanary." Technically she doesn't ask a question, so I don't immediately feel compelled to answer. I'm also calculat-ing if I think it's a good or a bad thing that she is asking me. She doesn't seem mad. She seems happy. She seems like she knows she's been wrong and now she knows the truth. I don't think I'm going to get arrested for leaving notes in the White House or anything like that. She rephrases her thought.

"Simone, are you @queencanary?" Memories of the past few weeks march through my mind like a parade. I see the things I've been thinking, doing, hoping for, working towards. I see my friends, my family, my classmates. I think of the tweets and im-ages I've posted. I think of all the things I've learned that I had no idea about. I think about the horror of my dream The sweat, the tears, the fear. I think about the decision I made to do something about what I saw. No matter what. No matter the risks or the fact that people might think I'm even crazier than they already do. I am Queen Canary. I realize The President is still waiting for me to respond, although I'm pretty sure we all already know the answer to her question.

I have nothing to hide. I am proud of myself. I have used my voice and I have taken action. I've done all the things I said I would do to make sure that the world knows the truth about climate change, so that we can stop it. There is no hesitation or embarrassment in my voice when I answer her. I am confident. I am not ashamed.

"Yes, I am Queen Canary. I left the Post-its. All of them. I wrote all the posts. I did all the research. I have a mission. This may sound a little crazy to you, but I had a dream and my dreams are known to come true." I make apologetic eyes at Mr. Carpenter and Connelly. The encourage me to go on with their kind, forgiving smiles. I guess he's probably known for a long time now that I think about it. Between my parents, Khalil, and Connelly. "I dreamed that the world was about to die completely because of the climate crisis and I had to do something about it. I couldn't be silent. I didn't know what to do, so I went to a medium to get direction from the universe. Connelly's mom came through to me and told me that true love is the answer. Mr. Carpenter told me that the best way to fix the problem is to, well, get you to change your mind and understand the science. So I've been trying to do both. Get all of us to find true love because I didn't really know who she meant, and try to get you to believe the science."

There. It's all out. I feel free. Elated. Proud. Nervous. I feel forgiveness. In myself. For myself. By myself. Happy, joyful, cleansing tears fill my eyes. I don't blink them back. I let them fall. I have nothing to hide. I've done a good job. I've done what I needed to do. I didn't give up. I did hard, brave things. I stand up straight and with my shoulders pulled back. I think of how I saw myself in the mirror before homecoming. I like the strength that I saw, the confidence. Axl may have tried to take a piece of that girl with him, but he didn't. She's still here and she's telling the President of the United States how she's changing the world.

"Well, excellent. I would like to thank you for your dedication to educating others about the truths of the climate crisis, including myself. I found your work to be very helpful as I looked for information on my own rather than depending on the criminals who filled my cabinet. I'm so embarrassed that I did not see through them. I was oblivious to their plans to hurt children and our planet, and I'm going to fix that. This morning as I watched the newscasts from around the country, I was overwhelmed with how much love I witnessed. Even though bad things happen every day, there is so much goodness in this world. It's my job to protect it, to make sure that all of the students I saw on television today and all the ones I haven't met yet have a safe place to learn, grow, and live out their lives. You did what you set out to do, Simone, Queen Canary, you helped the world find true love. True love is home, family, nature, kindness, conviction, courage, and sacrifice. Your campaign has shown what is great about this country."

I'm full of pride and relief. I've never been so happy. I notice my mom and dad have come back into the room to check on us. She's standing next to Mr. Carpenter. He lays a hand on her shoulder.

"Thank you. I did what I had to do. Now you are going to do what you have to do. I've learned the hard way how much it hurts when you stay quiet when you should speak up. I'm proud of myself for saying what I need to say. I still need to come clean though. I don't want to stand behind Queen Canary anymore. What you're going to do Madame President is really brave. It's admitting you're wrong and making it right. I want to be brave too." The President speaks with her natural confidence, "That you already are, Simone. You have accomplished many courageous things already. Your bravery has inspired courage in many others. I have a few ideas and updates that I would like to share with you." I nod eagerly for her to go ahead.

"In addition to your protests this morning, an article ran in The Post. It is getting quite a bit of attention from my colleagues as well as citizens across the nation and the world. In fact, an attorney, someone you know for that matter, is filing a lawsuit against the government. Your friend, Khalil, is it? His father is going to defend Mother Earth and attempt to prosecute the people who have been harming her. He will be focusing his efforts on politicians and business people who are allowing their greed to override their humanity. He has been working on this project for some time now, and it appears that he is choosing now as the right time to move forward. That is due to the work that you have done. You have created a movement with momentum, Simone. Mr. Williams has had some help from

Drew, eh, Mr. Carpenter. They have been putting together a case. They have had some additional helpers as well." She pauses to let me brain catch up to what she's saying. She lifts her eyes and catches the gaze of Mr. Carpenter, my mom, and my dad. I want to ask a question. I want to know more of what that might mean, but my mom speaks up.

"Simone Alice Marker," she begins in barely a whisper. I instinctively tilt my head towards her to hear her better. "I have something else to tell you. I'm sure this is all very overwhelming to you. I'm sorry for springing this on you right now, but there really is no time like the present. I, um, I, I am @undercoverearthmom1965. I sent you the link to the school conspiracy report."

"YOU WHAT? MOM! What? Are you serious?" I'm not mad; I am shocked. My mom? My mom the nurse who takes care of sick people day in and day out? The one who believes the environment makes them sicker? The woman who is ticked off about the climate crisis every day? Oh. Well, actually that makes more sense when I say it like that. She takes a few steps towards me. My jaw is on the ground. My mom is a bad-ass. "How did you get it? What?" Now my brain really can't catch up.

"After Mrs. Carpenter died and I kept seeing the same environmental illnesses occurring in my patients, I got scared and upset. I didn't know what to do, so I did a lot of research. Mr. Carpenter, Mr. Williams, and me, we were like a team. We pooled our resources and connections and decided to figure this out. To figure out what to do about this mess that we are in. When you had your dream, and you could clearly see the future of the planet, I knew that you could lead us. Even when you weren't ready to tell us, I already knew. Dr. A reached out to me. She was very worried and you hadn't yet fulfilled your promise to tell us. I went ahead and reached out to you with the report to encourage you to ask for help. She did what she had to do," I'm surprised Dr. A told her, but I'm not mad. I understand. She needed to protect my mental health first. My mom keeps talking.

"I knew you could be the spark. I knew how important it would be for you to speak, to use your voice, and take action on what you saw. I wasn't quite sure how to approach the situation. Maybe I should have told you sooner, but I saw something in you Simone that I wanted you to own. I wanted you to know your power and your strength. You have skills that we don't have. Shoot, you know how to use Tweeter or whatever its called. Your passion and energy were a sight to behold. I wanted to support you but needed your leadership."

I stare at her in amazement. My mom sat back so that I could lead the way? Me? "I hope you're not mad. I just knew you could do it in ways that I couldn't. We are all so proud of what you have accomplished."

"Mom, I'm not mad. I'm proud of you too. It takes all of us in our own ways with our own talents to make a difference. That report got a lot of people's attention, including mine. I'm not mad, Mom," I repeat so she knows I'm sure. It makes sense though. They had a guy on the inside, Mr. Carpenter. He could easily get classified materials related to the environment, but he couldn't very well leak them himself.

My dad gets a word in. "You did good, my Queen Canary. I'm very proud of you. You were thoughtful and action-oriented. You looked for facts and asked for help. You took care of yourself. I was worried about you. We were keeping a close eye on your health. That was the most important thing to us. You managed it all so beautifully. Expect maybe your pre-cal grade. I got your recent progress report." He frowns dramatically. I think he's kidding. He's got to be kidding, right?

I'm overcome with joy and support. We did it. I still really want to host the protest this weekend. I'm not sure how that will work. "There's something else. I'm planning a big rally for Sunday at The Mall. Is that still okay?"

"Yes, I have heard about your planned protest for Sunday," the President answers me. "It is fine for you to proceed.

The war is not won yet. I have quite a bit of undoing to do, and it will take some heavy-hitting and ongoing efforts. That is one of items I wanted to pose to you today." She looks at me and Connelly. "I am wondering if your and you and your friends, Connelly of course, and, Khalil, perhaps some others you know, if you would lead a youth think tank and activism program on behalf of Mother Earth and all her children. Create a local committee that you can meet with face to face and then you can grow it nationally and worldwide."

"Hell, yeah!" I shout. My mom gives me The Look. I save the world and still she doesn't like a curse word. Mom's gonna mom. "One thing though, I want to come out as Queen Canary first. I'm actually thinking about maybe doing it on Sunday, at the rally. Maybe I could take the mic for a while to lead some chants and organize people, and maybe I could announce it there. And then after that, I can just be myself and Queen Canary online and stuff. What do you think? I just want to be me." *Murl*

The President speaks again, "I have an idea. I think it will be difficult to have a special moment at the rally because a according to my Secret Service, there are going to be thousands of people there. What if you, your new committee, and I hold a press conference together after the protest? Two things can occur simultaneously. I will admit the wrongdoings of the cabinet and other businesses and government leaders. I will announce the lawsuit that Mr. Williams is filing against those criminals. I will confess my own role in this outrage. I will explain that I trusted the wrong people. I made decisions based on bad data. I will explain that, now, I have surrounded myself with the facts, the science, and people who tell the truth. I will tell the world that I have changed, and that I own the mistakes I have made. I will assure them that I am going to make them right. I will outline a plan that Drew and I have made to right the climate wrongs. You, can tell the world who you are and introduce your committee. You can tell them as much or as little about you and how you came up with Queen Canary."

"Woah," I say. She's serious, which is good. That's the whole point, but a press conference! Like in the Blue Room? Like on TV? I hadn't pictured that. The adults are looking at me. Each of their faces with a unique expression. Mom looks anxious and proud. Dad looks protective and impressed. Mr. Carpenter looks like a love struck lunatic. I don't even know if he's paying any attention at all to what is happening. The President looks humble, determined, and focused. I turn to get a better look at Connelly. She hasn't said anything. She looks dumbstruck. She's got a lot absorb. I'm still worried about her. I think we've got a good plan for getting her back to herself. Dump Zach. Honesty with her dad. Spend more time together. Still. This is all a lot. They are waiting for me to respond to The President's proposal. I speak to Connelly first.

"Connelly, I want to do this, but I don't want to do it without you. Are you up for being on the committee? Are you up for a PRESS CONFERENCE?" My voice is gentle and enthusiastic. I need her. She takes my hand in her soft, shiny manicured one. "I'm ready, Simone. I'm ready to be the kind of friend I am meant to be. I think this will be good for me. I've felt trapped since mom died." She cuts her eyes pointedly at The President. A fierce but also forgiving look. My Connelly. She is the best person. She continues, "I've not fully understood your dreams or your determination. It was hard for me to think about the reality of it when I knew the reality of what happened with my mom. It was just too much to consider that what happened to her would happen to us all. You know what I mean?"

I nod. Yes, I know what she means. The weight of the climate crisis and the dream have been suffocating at times. That's why I had to be different. I couldn't just lie there under the weight. I had to move and speak. I know what she means. "So, yeah, I want to do something. I want to be part of the solution. I want to help." She hugs me tightly. It feels good to have my girl back.

"Okay, that's awesome because here's what I want to do.

I want to tell the whole truth. I want to tell people about my dreams, and how because of the way my mind works, because of all it can do, that sometimes all that energy and thinking and analyzing and intuiting can make me anxious or even depressed. I want to make sure kids know that they don't have to be so normal all the time. They can be themselves. If they have a thing like mine, like a sixth sense or whatever, it's cool—it's not weird. If their brain works differently than the average person, that's great because their brain is probably going to do really dope things. I've been trying so hard to fit in and act normal that I think I've been missing out on who I really am. Like all of who I am if that makes sense. I want to get up there and be like, *Hey kids-I'm a weirdo. I'm a psychic. And it's hard and all but I love it, and I'm doing pretty awesome things with it, like helping to save the world. And you can too! You do you! If you're normal. Be normal. If you're not, which my guess is most kids aren't, then be that.*"

This gets a chuckle. I think it is my cavalier delivery and not really the words. The words are true. We spend so much time trying to be who we think we should be that no one knows the real person they are trying to impress or convince. That seems like a lot of wasted energy resulting in no one just being who they are. They get it. I got a hunch this doesn't just get automatically better when you get out of high school. Seems to me it might be an ongoing thing. I see my mom and dad reach for each other's hands. They are cute. It's agreed upon. We have a plan. After the rally, we will meet The President's Secret Service agents at the White House Visitor Center and then we will go from there to the Briefing room.

It's time to end this party. The President and Mr. Carpenter need to get back to the White House. They apparently have a lot of work to do. There are a lot of hugs and some more tears. Laughter too though. Connelly is staying with me. We are going to plan details for the rally and start brainstorming the committee members and work. The President is about to walk out the door when I remember something that I have been dying to ask her the whole time. "Wait, Madame President." She replies, "You can call me Naomi in situations like this, Simone." I cannot, my mom would kick my butt. I just nod and go on. "I have one more question for you."

"Go ahead."

"The Post-it, the one with Mr. Carpenter's number on it, was that why you two got together?"

She throws her head back and exposes her thin, almond colored neck. It's an oddly intimate gesture. She laughs a hearty but airy laugh. I'm not sure what to make of it.

"Oh, Simone. I got such a kick out of that Post-it. Drew and I almost immediately fell for one another. He had me from the get go. I was in interested in knowing him better from the moment he re-introduced himself to me on September 11 after my speech. Not many people speak to me like that. By the time I found the Post-it, I had already figured out the mystery of all the other ones. I figured it was you. I did not know why, yet, of course, but I figured you had your reasons. Now, I know. We got a wonderful kick out of it. I keep it on my desk. It makes me smile."

I'm peculiarly disappointed at this information, but all's well that ends well, I suppose. I shrug and smile at her. My face is goofy; I can feel it. I don't care though and neither does she.

"You are a darling. Thank you for everything you have done."

CHAPTER TWENTY-ONE

Sunday, September 29th

The day of the rally, the sun is shining and there's the first hint of true fall in the air. I'm up super early, and even though I'm excited, the 4:00 AM wake-up call is brutal. The whole gang is meeting at my house to take the train into the city. Mom and dad. Mr. Carpenter and Connelly. Mr. and Mrs. Williams with Khalil and Khori. Even Principal Aguilera and Miss Starnes. We are getting ready to leave for the station. We have all sorts of supplies between us. Signs, posters, banners, snacks, waters, portable phone chargers, megaphones, bull-horns, and noisemakers galore. I want to bring Cherry Garcia and mom says hell to the no. Well, she says no, but it was firm.

We are getting ready to leave when a light blue Prius pulls up hot in the driveway. Out bounces Moriah. And then Melia. I'm assuming because it looks just like her. Moriah is wearing a bad-ass baby blue track suit and smoke colored J's. She's got matching baby blue beads stacked at the ends of her braids. Melia is wearing ripped jeans, grass green Vans, and a cropped T-shirt with the Ninja Turtles holding up a brightly colored Earth between them. Well I'll be darned. When they said we had stuff in common, they weren't joking. I can't look away. She's got her braids gathered together at the base of her neck. Her striking face exposed and open. Long, dangly gold earrings hang to her shoulders. She's got a matching stack of bangles snaking up her arm.

"We're here! Wait for us," Moriah shouts as she pulls Melia by the hand. Melia is holding an armful of signs. Moriah runs towards Khalil and gives him a huge hug. She's calling out polite and enthusiastic *hellos* to all the adults. She stops at me and gives me the same sort of hug. "Hi! Congratulations. This is so rad!" She is a refreshing, light, airy breeze. I bet she's never met anyone that didn't love her instantly. You have no choice. Even I liked her when I went to tell her man I wanted to love him. I laugh at myself. If Moriah is wind, Melia is still water. She's shaken free of Moriah's hand and is steadily making her way to the group. No rushing. No shouting. Confident and calm. She smiles and nods at everyone. She seems shy but not self-conscious. Moriah introduces her to everyone first and once she does, everyone begins filing into cars and shouting out last minute details. It's busy and loud as everyone tries to figure out who is riding with whom. Khori also got his hands on a noise-maker, so there's that incessant noisy nonsense.

Moriah presents Melia to me last. "Simone, this is Melia! Remember, I was telling you about her. I hope its okay that we came together. Khail said the more the merrier." She pushes Melia to me. Melia gives her a look. It's the *stand down* look. I know it from giving it to my Guilt Dragon.

"Hi," she says without emotion. Just even. Still water.

"Hi," suddenly my brain goes to black. I can't think of anything else to say. I am staring at her like I can't take her in fast enough. I scan my body like Dr. A taught me to. What is happening here? My brain is flat. My stomach is a damn butterfly garden. My palms are sweating enough to water said butterfly garden. And I'm just standing there smiling like an idiot.

"Hi," she says again expect for now she's smiling. She

reaches out her hand to shake mine. Like a proper grown up. I extend mine towards her. A zip of electricity shocks my hand when it touches hers. I apologize. "Oh, god, sorry. Must be static." That makes no sense. There's no static out here. I don't even have on long sleeves for it to be caught in.

"It's not. It's not static, I mean." She says calmly. Knowingly. I stare back at her. Holy shit. My insides heat up. A warming starts below my belly button and spreads down through my legs, settling in my toes. There's an energy in them that makes me feel like with one little bounce, I could fly. I could fly away. I could fly away with Melia. The warmth springs from my toes and makes its way back up my body. It settles in my chest and surrounds my heart like a hug. Then I feel it color my cheeks. She watches me. It's like she can see the warm energy lighting up an option that I didn't even know I had. I take a step back. I feel different. I'm not sure what's happening. Or am I? Am I the most sure I've ever been? My life with boys and dates and kisses and touches wanted and unwanted flash through my mind as if I'm about to die. But I'm not dying, I'm coming to life.

"Wanna keep holdin' my hand?" She drawls. I hadn't realized that I was still holding on. I do. With her save the planet posters in one hand and mine in the other, we join Connelly in the back of my mom's navy Accord. They are both looking at me with love. True love.

THE END

Thank you for reading my novel.

Your feedback is important to me. I read every review in hopes of getting better so that I can keep doing the thing that I love.

Please leave a review of my work.

Thank you so much. You are the top notch.

Happy radical reading to you. XO.

Tara

Made in the USA
Lexington, KY
15 December 2019